NEW YORK REVIEW BOOKS
CLASSICS

BALCONY IN THE FOREST

JULIEN GRACQ (1910–2007) was born Louis Poirier in Saint-Florent-le-Vieil, a small village in western France. An excellent student and a voracious reader, he studied in Paris in the early 1930s, where he encountered the work of André Breton and the surrealists. His first book, *Au Château d'Argol* (*The Castle of Argol*, 1938) was praised by Breton as the first surrealist novel. In 1940, as a lieutenant in the French army, Gracq was captured by the Germans and sent to a prisoner-of-war camp in Silesia. Following the war and his release, he became a geography and history teacher at a lycée in Paris, where he remained for more than twenty years. He taught as Louis Poirier and wrote as Julien Gracq, a name that combined his favorite Stendhal character, Julien Sorel, and the Roman Gracchus brothers. Opposed to publicity and self-promotion, Gracq declined three requests from François Mitterand to dine at the president's residence and refused the Prix Goncourt when he was awarded it for his 1951 novel *Le Rivage des Syrtes* (*The Opposing Shore*). Unmarried, in 1970 he retired from teaching and returned to his hometown, where he lived with his sister until her death in 1996. He continued writing throughout his life, publishing novels, plays, poetry, and literary criticism.

RICHARD HOWARD is the author of seventeen volumes of poetry and has published more than one hundred fifty translations from the French, including, for NYRB, Marc Fumaroli's *When the World Spoke French*, Balzac's *Unknown Masterpiece*, and Maupassant's *Alien Hearts*. He has received a National Book Award for his translation of *Les Fleurs du mal* and a Pulitzer Prize for *Untitled Subjects*, a collection of poetry.

BALCONY IN THE FOREST

JULIEN GRACQ

Translated from the French and with a foreword by
RICHARD HOWARD

NEW YORK REVIEW BOOKS

New York

THIS IS A NEW YORK REVIEW BOOK
PUBLISHED BY THE NEW YORK REVIEW OF BOOKS
435 Hudson Street, New York, NY 10014
www.nyrb.com

Published in French as *Un Balcon en forêt* by Éditions Corti.
Translation published by arrangement with The Permissions Company, Inc., on
behalf of George Braziller, Inc.

Library of Congress Cataloging-in-Publication Data
Names: Gracq, Julien, 1910–2007, author. | Howard, Richard, translator.
Title: Balcony in the forest / Julien Gracq ; translated and with a foreword by
   Richard Howard.
Other titles: Balcon en forêt. English
Description: New York : NYRB Classics, 2017.
Identifiers: LCCN 2017024489| ISBN 9781681371399 (paperback) | ISBN
   9781681371405 (epub)
Subjects: LCSH: World War, 1939-1945—Fiction. | BISAC: FICTION / War &
   Military. | FICTION / Psychological. | FICTION / Literary. | GSAFD: War
   stories. | Love stories.
Classification: LCC PQ2613.R124 B3513 2017 | DDC 843/.914—dc23
LC record available at https://lccn.loc.gov/2017024489

ISBN 978-1-68137-139-9
Available as an electronic book; ISBN 978-1-68137-140-5

Printed in the United States of America on acid-free paper.
10 9 8 7 6 5 4 3 2 1

TRANSLATOR'S FOREWORD

NEITHER document nor testimony (Gracq's own experiences in World War II were on an entirely different front, and in altogether other circumstances), *Balcony in the Forest*, Gracq's fourth novel, and actually the *precipitate* of the encounter between a certain historical situation, one that was very unstable and indeed fugitive, and the inclination of the author's fantasy, is the only one of this author's fictions—among so many legends, romances, *gestes*—which can be presumed to be realistic. In the little forest outpost at the beginning of World War II, Lieutenant Grange has a passionate yet detached affair, during the fall and winter months, with Mona, a lovely child-widow whom he encounters in the forest much the way Golaud encounters Mélisande. Then spring comes, and with it the murderous reality of the German avalanche. History, for an interval, becomes a kind of pure awaiting, in which Gracq is enabled to feel, for the first time, what he calls "imaginative communication with reality." All his other novels—*The Castle of Argol* (1938), *A Dark Stranger* (1945), and *The Opposing Shore* (1951, translated in 1986)—are so many myths of abeyance and interregnum in which the characters, or rather the *figures* (as we might say of any human silhouettes moving in darkness against a sanguinary light, within a singular silence) expunge each other's energies during a period of suspense, of transgressive daring, until the Unspeakable Event engulfs them in a longed-for yet deferred catastrophe. For this novelist has what might be called a Parsifal Complex (indeed, *Balcony in the Forest* opens with the adjuration by which Gurnemanz begins that music-drama: "Forest Guardians, guardians of sleep as well—waken at least with the dawn!"), an imagination so structured that any action is merely the delusive interlude, the masque of misapprehension, before a ravaging revelation. For Gracq, of course, the Grail is indeed revealed as a cup of trembling, a ruinous chalice—but perhaps we never did put much credence in Wagner's stagey salvation. Hadn't Nietzsche warned us that with Amfortas, with Kundry, with Parsifal himself, we were only two steps away from the hospital? The astonishing thing about Gracq's novel, the last full-length fiction he was to write (in 1958, some eighteen years after the occurrences it is concerned to adumbrate), is that it has been able to transcribe in terms of contemporary life, of contemporary death, precisely those images and incidents which in all of Gracq's other works are assigned the distancing labels "gothic" or "surreal" or certainly "magical." Such a transformation has come about not because Gracq has changed—for he has not: no novelist ever remained so true to his esoteric inspirations as Monsieur Poirier, a geography professor who chooses to create his poems, his play, his essays, and his fictions, even his translation of Kleist's *Penthesilea* and his study of André Breton, under that mysterious, Breton-sounding pseudonym *Gracq*. But because reality changed.

In English we called it the "phony war." In France it was called, with varying degrees of validity, the *drôle de guerre*. For nine months after the declaration of war between Germany and the Allies, hostilities were suspended, were not engaged. And in that gestation, there was a great silence, a terrible holding of a continent's breath until the blow fell in the easy June of 1940, and France fell with it, as if there were no such fierce thing as combat—only surrender, only collapse, only defeat. But in the bated September of 1939 there was no knowing, no telling: the mobilized troops were sent to the various frontiers—those famous and "impregnable" lines that were to be so readily erased—where they waited in a demoralizing silence for month after month. This is the interval Gracq chose; it took him nearly two decades to write his way into it, to let reality speak in the terms of his somber enchantment. As he says:

> Things were suspended, but there was no clearing, no perspective. It was not impossible (or so people thought) that things might end without hostilities. There might, then, be a "white" peace. And there were also all kinds of catastrophic possibilities, including

the one that came to pass. We found ourselves, truly, on the brink of a sort of mist-filled chasm, out of which it was very difficult to see what would emerge. It is, I think, quite an *original* situation, that of a declared war that does not get itself fought, that cannot begin.

Hence it is this novel of the phony war, of the inauthentic peace and the inactual hostilities, which is the least oneiric of Gracq's works. It is the least oneiric *book* because the period it treats was itself a kind of waking dream. The France of 1939 and 1940 was living as if there had been no military necessity. "There was," Gracq observed in 1971, "the sentiment of a void, the sense of an enormous blank. Nothing occurred: there was an utterly somnambulistic aspect to everything. For everything continued as if nothing had happened. There was a paralysis, a putting-in-parenthesis, a prelude—to what? No one knew. It was *pure anticipation*." The story of Lieutenant Grange (*lieu-tenant*, place-saving: even his rank is a kind of mystery, a holding action), assigned to command the isolated French blockhouse at Hautes Falizes, in the middle of the forest—the Forest of Arden!—and, closer still, the Ardennes of the last Great War, near the Belgian border and the Meuse river. The story of Lieutenant Grange is nothing but the story of Anyman in a vacant moment whereof the true occurrences are the vast metamorphoses of nature (the turn of the seasons, the sullen erosion of rock to sand, the woodland murmurs of sprouting and decay), and the miniscule transformations within a single body ("When he put his weight on his heel, a sharp spear of pain leaped up to his hips. . . . Against the harsh cloth that bound his skin, he felt the faint velvety shudder of fever, still almost voluptuous").

It is of interest to note that this is Gracq's one novel to have been "made into" a movie, whereas *The Opposing Shore*, for example, has been produced as an opera: opera is of course the apposite "realization" for Gracq's work. Yet in the film of *Balcony in the Forest*, the author was amused to discover that the soldiers, the *other soldiers*, have much more continuous presence than in his book itself, though that presence has no effect on the process of the narrative. "Simply," as Gracq is pleased to say, "because in a scene in a novel, a character about whom the author has ceased to speak immediately becomes an *absent presence*, while in the film such a character remains caught in the camera field—he is still *there*." Gracq was astonished to find *the others* dragged into the visual field, for in his text, his imaginative substance, there are never others unless they are *named*, unless they are audible as language. However capital the images, however striking the visions, Gracq is the purest of novelists, and there is a sense in which he cannot be reduced, transferred, or even translated into other versions, other forms of art.

He can, of course, be translated, in the absolute sense; the coincidence of Gracq's privileged fantasmatics with an actual historical sequence affords his (third) translator a particular opportunity, one of which Gracq himself appears to be quite conscious, as in this passage where Lieutenant Grange studies a pamphlet describing the German offensive weapons:

The ponderous gray silhouettes ... seemed curiously exotic—another world—with their simultaneously baroque, theatrical and sinister quality of German war machines which, despite all the requirements of technology, still managed to remind him of Fafnir. "*Unheimlich*," he thought: there was no French word; he studied them with a mixture of repugnance and fascination. Outside, the heavy rain of the Ardennes was beginning to fall with the darkness, its drumming muffled by the snow. Unconsciously, he strained to hear the occasional noises from the crew room, afraid of being surprised, as if he were poring over obscene photographs.

Grange, then, is a kind of Amfortas, a Fisher King (the title of Gracq's play of 1948), wishing for, yet reading against, the arrival of the Germans. As Kundry says: *I await the conqueror.* "Never before," muses Grange as he wonders over the war's suspension, "never before had France pulled the sheet over her head with this feverish hand, this taste of nausea in her mouth." And what a boon to the translator of 1958, then, in what became the novel's final sentence, suggesting the kind of overdetermined, lyric necessity of this musical, mysterious text: "He lay for a moment more with his eyes wide open in the darkness.... Then he pulled the blanket up over his head and went to sleep."

—RICHARD HOWARD
1987

BALCONY IN THE FOREST

He! ho! Waldhuter ihr
Schlafhuter mitsammen
So wacht doch mindest am Morgen.

Heigh! Ho! Forest Guardians!
Guardians of Sleep as well—
Waken at least with the dawn.

WAGNER: Parsifal

EVER since his train had outdistanced the smoke and the suburbs of Charleville, it seemed to Lieutenant Grange that the world's ugliness was disappearing with them: he discovered there was no longer a single house in sight. The train, following the slow river's course, had at first plunged between the gentle slopes of wooded hills. Then, at each bend of the river, the valley had grown deeper, while the train's racket echoed from the empty cliffs and a raw wind, already piercing in the late autumn afternoon, scoured his face when he put his head out the compartment door. The track changed banks capriciously, crossing the Meuse on single-span bridges of iron girders, suddenly rushing into short tunnels across the neck of a bend. Each time the valley reappeared, its poplars shimmering in the golden light, the gorge seemed deeper between its forest curtains and the Meuse seemed slower and darker, as if it had been flowing over a bed of rotten leaves.

The train was empty: it appeared to serve these solitudes for the mere pleasure of passing through the cool evening, running between slopes of yellow woodland that reached ever higher into the clear blue October afternoon; at the river's edge, the trees revealed only a narrow ribbon of meadow, as smooth as an English lawn.

"A train for the *Domain of Arnheim*," thought the lieutenant, a great Poe enthusiast, and as he lit a cigarette he leaned his head back against the serge upholstery so his gaze could follow the crest of the high, shaggy cliffs aureoled by the low sun. Down the sudden corridors of tributary gorges, the distant foliage vanished behind a haze as blue as cigar smoke; you felt that the earth was crimped beneath this thick and knotty forest as naturally as a Negro's scalp. Yet even here ugliness was not to be forgotten altogether: from time to time the train stopped at scaling, mud-colored little stations that clung to the embankment between the river and the cliff; against the military blue of the already dim windowpanes, soldiers in khaki were dozing on the mail wagons —then the green valley grew almost desolate for a moment: the train passed lugubrious yellow houses sliced out of the earth and apparently powdering the surrounding greenness with dust from the gypsum quarries—and, when his disillusioned gaze returned to the Meuse, it now discerned here and there the jerry-built cabins of raw brick and concrete, and along the bank the barbwire emplacements where the river's spate had hung a litter of rotten weeds: even before the first cannonfire, the war's rust and ruin, its odor of scorched earth, its spoiled wasteland, had already dishonored this still intact canton of luxuriant Gaul.

When he got off at the Moriarmé station, the shadow of the enormous cliff was already darkening the little town; it had suddenly grown cold; a siren roared in his ears at point-blank range, and he felt a cold shudder run down his back, but it was only a factory whistle that released a dreary crowd of North African workers into the little square. He remembered how during his vacation, at night, he sometimes strained to hear the town fire-engine's siren: one blast was a flue fire, two a fire in the village, three a fire on a remote farm. The third blast produced a sigh of relief at many windows. "Here it would be just the reverse," he thought: "one blast for peace, three for bombs—what matters is to know how to tell the difference." Everything in this war turned out oddly. He had the stationmaster show him where the regimental combat post was. Now he was strolling down a wretched gray street that descended to the Meuse; the sudden October twilight soon emptied it of civilians, but everywhere from the yellow house fronts leaked a murmur of soldiery: the clank of helmets and messkits, the clatter of hobnailed boots on tiles: "if you close your eyes for a second," Grange thought, "a modern regiment makes more racket than all the armor of the Hundred Years' War."

The command post was at the river's edge, a dingy, suburban pavilion separated from the quay by a railing and a starved-looking flower bed already trampled by soldiers, where motorcycles leaned against the naked stalks of the lilac bushes: two months of billeting had scratched the corridor floor and walls to the raw wood as high as a man could reach, like a hive's too-narrow entrance. Grange waited for some time in a dusty room where a typewriter clattered in the half-darkness, the shutters only partly folded back: occasionally the quartermaster sergeant, without raising his head, stubbed out a cigarette against a corner of the drafting table: originally the pavilion must have been the foundry engineer's office. Between the shutters, the wall of trees seemed pasted against the window from the ceiling down to the Meuse, which looked very dark now alongside its slag bank; from time to time cries of children rose from the street, muffled by the war's weight and insignificant as a rabbit's screams. When he clicked his heels in the colonel's office, light still, Grange was struck by the look in the man's sea-gray eyes and the lipless mouth beneath the hard bristles of his mustache: the colonel looked like von Moltke. There was a lunge of abrupt and piercing life in that look, then the eyes were immediately veiled by a kind of whitish film and withdrew under the heavy lids; the expression became that of fatigue, but cunning withal, and concessive: behind this hooded falcon's immobility, the talons were clearly in readiness.

Grange handed over his orders specifying his final destination; the colonel checked his schedule. In front of him lay several sheets which he indifferently brushed aside. Grange sensed that these papers concerned himself: there was probably a dossier on him in the files of military security.

"I'm assigning you to the blockhouse at Hautes Falizes," the colonel said a few seconds later, still speaking in the neutral tone of the service—yet he communicated a secret intention to his words, for his eyes momentarily contracted to hard points. "You will go up there tomorrow morning with Captain Vignaud. As for today, you'll mess with the quartermaster corps."

Grange regarded a dinner with the corps as less than promising; launched into this war that had started so quietly, at the zero point, he did not dream of flinching before whatever task might be asked of him, but he did not *participate*—instinctively, whenever possible, he kept his reserve and a certain distance. When he had left his gear in the truck that was to take him up to Les Falizes, he ordered some ham and eggs in a worker's cafe whose shutters were drawn early, and then, crossing streets already immured and echoing to the march of patrols, he reached his quarters for the night.

The room was a rather narrow attic whose windows overlooked the Meuse; in the corner opposite the iron bed some fruit was drying on an old newspaper spread over a rickety commode: the insistent, sweetish odor of the crab-apples were so strong that he suddenly felt sick. He opened the windows wide and sat down on a trunk, completely disenchanted. The sheets, the blankets smelled of rotten apples, like an old cider press; he pulled the bed in front of the open window. The candle flame trembled in the slow draft of air from the river; between the eaves, he could see the heavy slabs of the Meuse floor, the schist a strange wine-lees color. He undressed, his mood extremely somber: this foundry town, these sooty back-streets, the colonel, the apples, everything in this initiation to a billeted life, was distasteful to him.

"A *blockhouse*," he wondered, "what does that mean?" He ransacked his already remote memory of the regulations concerning campaign fortifications: no, he could recall nothing at all. It must be under the code of military justice instead; the word itself offered him little reassurance, reminding him of both a house of detention and a prison block. When he had blown out the candle, everything changed. Lying on his side, his gaze plunged down over the Meuse; the moon had risen above the cliff; the only sound was the calm murmur of water slipping over a submerged weir and the cries of the screech owls perched quite near him, in the trees on the opposite bank. The little town had vanished with its smoke; the odor of the great forests glided off the cliffs with the fog and drowned it to the depths of its factory alleys; nothing was left save the starry night and around him these miles and miles of forest. The afternoon's enchantment returned. Grange realized that half his life was going to be restored to him: in wartime, the night is inhabited. "Under the stars . . ." he mused, and thought vaguely of narrow white roads beneath the moon, the round apple trees in black pools of shadow, tents pitched in woods full of wild animals and surprises. He fell asleep, one hand hanging out of his bed over the Meuse as if across the gunwale of a boat: tomorrow was already very far away.

As SOON as they had passed the last houses of Mori-armé, the tar pavement stopped and they began taking the first zigzag turns. It was as if the stony roadbed had been plowed up for its whole width, becoming a kind of Saharan *reg,* a river of pebbles with neither gutter nor shoulder between the two walls of trees. Grange consulted his map between jolts: they were getting into the forest part of the route. At each hairpin turn, the valley grew deeper, a wisp of fog appeared above the river which drained faster toward the delta now, quickened by eddies like water emptying from a bath. The morning was gay with sunlight, fresh and transparent, but Grange was amazed by the silence of these woods where no birds sang. Leaning out of the window, he half turned his back to the captain and raised himself on his arms to look down to the valley floor: no matter where he was, perspectives had always fascinated him to the point of rudeness. In the back of the truck there were two sacks of biscuits, a side of beef wrapped in a piece of jute sacking, a machine-gun tripod, and a few rolls of barbed wire.

"Let's stop a minute at l'Eclaterie, since this is your first time up," Captain Vignaud said, smiling. "The view is worth the trouble."

Almost at the top of the slope, a small roadside platform furnished with two benches had been built out over the valley. From here you could see the summit of the somewhat lower opposite slope and the woods stretching to the horizon, thick and matted like a wolfskin, enormous as a stormy sky. At his feet there was the slow, slender Meuse, fettered by the distance to its floor, and Moriarmé burrowed into the hollow of the huge forest shell like an ant lion at the bottom of its pit. The town consisted of three convex streets that followed the meander's curve, and ran in terraces above the Meuse like contour lines; between the lowest street and the river a block of houses had disappeared, leaving an empty oblong barred in the slanting light by a sundial's neat gnomon: the church square. The whole landscape, its ample masses of shadow, its thread of open meadows perfectly legible, had a dry and military precision, an almost geodetic beauty: these eastern sectors were made for war, Grange thought. He had been on maneuvers only in the jumbled west, where even the trees were never quite round, never quite vertical.

"That certainly looks like a good, clean cut," he said politely: the captain was wearing a staff-college ribbon.

The captain shook out his pipe with a look of disgust. "The front is thirty kilometers long, the river's sixty," he said abruptly. "A line like that eats up everything."

Grange felt like a novice: he must have violated some taboo of the general-staff mess. They got back into the truck in silence.

The truck climbed quite slowly up the bumpy path. As soon as the zigzags stopped and they had lumbered onto the plateau, the truck turned into a straight road that seemed to run on through the underbrush as far as the eye could reach. The forest was stunted—the trees were mostly birches, dwarf beech, ash, and pin oaks, all gnarled like pear trees—but seemed extraordinarily dense, without a rent or clearing anywhere; on each side of the ribbon of river it was as if this earth had been shaggy with trees for all eternity, had exhausted ax and saber alike by the resurgence of its greedy fleece. Occasionally, a service path ran through the trees, as narrow as an animal trail. The solitude was complete, and yet the possibility of a meeting did not seem altogether unlikely; sometimes, in the distance, there seemed to be a man standing by the roadside in a long pilgrim's cape: at close range, this turned out to be a small fir, its shoulders black and square against the curtain of bright leaves.

The road they were on must have followed the plateau's watershed, for there was never the sound of a stream, though two or three times Grange noticed a stone trough, half-buried in a recess of trees, from which a thread of clear water ran: it added to the silence of the fairy-tale forest.

Where am I being taken, he wondered. He calculated that they must have gone a good twelve kilometers since leaving the Meuse: Belgium couldn't be far away. But his mind floated in a comfortable obscurity: he asked for nothing better than to go on driving through the calm morning, between these moist thickets that smelled of squirrels' nests and fresh mushrooms. As they were about to take a turn, the truck slowed down, then, all its springs protesting, plunged left beneath the branches across a grass-grown breach. Among the trees, Grange made out a house with a peculiar-looking silhouette as if a kind of Savoyard chalet were caught in the branches, fallen like a meteorite among these forgotten thickets.

"This is where you live," Captain Vignaud said.

THE Hautes Falizes blockhouse was one of a series constructed in the heart of the forest to prevent enemy armored units from penetrating into the Belgian Ardennes toward the Meuse line. The structure consisted of a squat concrete cube with an armored door opening at the rear onto a zigzag path across a small barbwire emplacement that surrounded the blockhouse like a cabbage patch. The concrete had been perfunctorily daubed with faded olive-green paint that smelled of mold: fungus growths encouraged by the suffocating heat of the undergrowth caused damp patches to suppurate on the sides, as if wet sheets had been hung there every day. Two embrasures pierced the front of the blockhouse: one, narrow, for a machine gun; the other, a little larger, for an anti-tank gun. On top of this squat cube, as if on a pedestal too small for it, rested the projecting story of a little house, entered from one side by a perforated iron staircase, like an American tenement fire escape: this was the quarters of the tiny garrison. Its ugliness was that of the poorest mining cabin or frontier hut; the dripping forest winters had pitted the exposed surfaces, torn off patches of plaster, and blackened the windows under the staircase with long streaks of rust that ran over onto the concrete. On cords hung under the eaves from the windows to the nearby branches, underwear and towels were drying. Against the blockhouse leaned the brand-new, galvanized-wire netting of a henroost and a crude plank rabbit hutch; tin cans that must have been thrown out of the windows and half-loaves of rotting bread were scattered all over the barbwire emplacement. The bizarre coupling of this prehistoric *mastaba* with a ramshackle suburban cottage, surrounded by such hobo's bric-a-brac in the heart of the forest, had something perfectly improbable about it. Through the open windows, a cast-iron throat was making the woods ring with a barroom song which broke off at the sound of the truck.

> *On va guincher dans tous les caboulots*
> *Sur le plancher des va-ches. . . .*

There was no doubt about it, Grange thought, this war wasn't beginning the way he had thought it would. There were all kinds of surprises. The men came down the staircase one by one, their boots clattering, buckling their belts—clumsy, circumspect, and squinting like suspicious Berber tribesmen at their new commanding officer.

FOR a long while Grange clung to the half-sleep that kept him tossing on his camp bed, though the dawn was already pale at every window; since childhood, no sensation had been so purely delicious: he was free, in sole command of this Little Red Riding Hood hut, lost in the heart of the wilderness. On the other side of his door, the placid bustle of a waking farm added to his happiness: he connected it with long-familiar sounds; for the first time, Grange realized with a shock of incredulous delight that he was going to live here—that perhaps the war had its desert islands. The forest branches brushed against his windowpanes. A heavy clatter shook the staircase; Grange jumped off his bed and looked out the window: two soldiers, Hervouët and Gourcuff, were already disappearing between the trees, straightening their rifles with a shrug of the shoulder, their overcoat collars raised against the piercing chill. Behind the partition, someone was stirring up the stove; the sound of tinware promised hot coffee.

He stretched out on his bed a minute, wrapped in his coat. The day was gray and overcast; an atmosphere of foggy mornings, the idleness of Sundays in the country, filled the blockhouse; and a silence, so rare in military life, falling at intervals between the sounds on the other side of the wall, settled down in the middle of the room like a contented cat. The cold itself was not uncomfortable; and even in their absence, he felt that the air here was stirred only by young and well-fed bodies. For a moment Grange stared vacantly at the pale fume his breath left on the air, then turned over and gave a perplexed chuckle: the notion that this was an *outpost* completely bewildered him. The orders Captain Vignaud had passed on to him were simple. In case of attack, the engineers would fall back to a position in front of Les Falizes and blow up the road. The mission of the blockhouse was to destroy the tanks trapped by this demolition and to provide information as to the enemy's movements. The enemy was to be halted "with no thought of retreat." An underground tunnel into the woods was supposed to permit the garrison to leave the blockhouse without being seen and, in the last extremity, to withdraw toward the Meuse through the forest.

On the general-staff map, hanging down over the edge

of his table, he could see from his bed the route of orderly withdrawal which Captain Vignaud had drawn in red pencil, and which he was to start reconnoitering today. But his imagination found little stimulus in these improbable events. In front of him he had the woods reaching to the horizon, and then beyond that came the sheltering corner of Belgium that dropped down like a fold of curtain. The war was little by little falling asleep, the army yawning like a class that has handed in its papers, waiting for the bell and the end of maneuvers. Nothing would happen. Perhaps nothing would happen. Grange leafed absent-mindedly through the file of official communications, the combat orders, the munitions accounts: a fine rain of learned paragraphs engendered by an ingenious and polemical madness, which seemed to take account of earthquakes in advance; then he put them in an envelope and locked them away in his drawer with a gesture that was an exorcism. Such things belonged to the order of events which, too minutely foreseen, did not happen. These were the notarized archives of the war; they slept here waiting for confirmation; reading these pages that tracked down the unpredictable from comma to comma, Grange felt inexpressibly reassured: it was as though the war were already over. A finger scratched at the door with a timidity surprising after the powerful racket of boots that had preceded it.

"Coffee, *mon yeutenant*."

Grange jumped off his bed and pulled on his boots: all the same, it wasn't an ordinary house. The iron-soled boots made a dull sound against the bare concrete, with no vibration or resonance, as if he were walking on a new road or a bridge abutment. Grange felt he was welded to that cool dark cavern underneath, which his ear unconsciously questioned—a snail *en promenade* outside its shell. And suddenly the fairy-tale house didn't quite reassure him any more. They slept here like sailors in the lull of hot nights, making for gray seas and trying to forget that the wind would be rising one of these days.

It SEEMED as if the rhythm of the blockhouse regime had been determined once and for all. It was something of a peasant life they led, slowly vegetating at one of the least sensitive nerve endings within the war's great body: the season, the wind, the rain, the moment's inclination, and the round of household tasks created much more of a stir than the general-staff bulletins, whose echoes died away on these somnolent frontiers as sluggishly as ripples on a beach. From this perspective it was easy to understand that the war depended on violent movements, like a man pulling himself out of a quicksand limb by limb: paralyzed as they were, the earth reclaimed them for its own, they sent down roots, the garrison returned to peasantry.

The blockhouse at Les Falizes sheltered a marginal clan like men living in isolated moorland shanties: as seldom seen in towns as highlanders in the valleys, living off the land by individual craft, half charcoal burners, half poachers. Four times a week, Hervouët and Gourcuff left for their *lumberyard*, a little clearing the division's engineers had made in the Braye forest two kilometers from Les Falizes; here stakes were cut for the barbwire emplacements being completed along the front. There was reason to believe the men cut few enough, for the Braye forest gullies were full of game, and allowances for the trip there and back were generously calculated during these shortening days. Often Grange, awake before daylight and musing in his bed, surprised a wary footstep on the dripping stairs: he knew it was Hervouët, a knapsack on his back, leaving with Gourcuff to make the rounds of his traps. Grange found he liked both men: their passion for outdoor living left him all the more time to himself, and he was pleased by their discretion and reserve, the silent manners of woodsmen and scouts accustomed to keeping their mouths closed and their ears open and not inclined to discuss private matters. Hervouët was tall and spare, a duckhunter from La Brière whom nights of lying in wait had made as day-blind as a cat. Gourcuff, an almost illiterate day laborer from Questembert, was stocky and redfaced: he was not a gifted man and his only natural aptitudes seemed to be those of a remarkable drinker. As in most such cases, the sedentary man had become the nomad's serf: Hervouët had pressed his seal on this soft wax—where everything he uttered was engraved as if it were scripture—and Gourcuff had become his sword-bearer, his beater, his hunt servant. When they slipped into the overgrown service paths, Hervouët, who liked having his arms free, would hang his rifle on Gourcuff's shoulder as if on a hat peg. They disappeared early in the morning between the trees, taciturn and long-striding, like the Amazon *seringueiros.*

"Where have Hervouët and Gourcuff gone this time?"

"They're at their yard, *mon yeutenant.* There's no more meat."

They emerged from the thickets at the afternoon's end, smelling of game and breathing hard, like wet dogs, their knapsacks full of dead animals, empty bottles, and Belgian cigarettes. They brought news as well, for these desolate forests, wakened by the war and full of hideouts and refuges, hummed louder than telegraph wires.

Once Hervouët and Gourcuff had gone, Corporal Olivon retired to the common room, engrossed in mysterious domestic tasks, and Grange had the whole day empty before him. Mornings, he usually read and wrote at the deal table in front of the foggy little window facing the forest, until the moment, every other day, when he heard the truck blowing its horn on the road up to Les Falizes, bringing supplies, mail, newspapers, various clandestine substances Olivon ordered from Moriarmé to "stuff" his chickens on, and occasionally materiel for the upkeep of the blockhouse and its nearby defenses:

cans of paint, pruning tools, cartridges for signals, or rolls of barbed wire. When Grange had signed the receipts, the curtain fell for two days more on the inhabited world: in this forest wilderness perched high above the Meuse, it was as if they were on a roof and the ladder taken away.

With two men requisitioned almost daily for wood-cutting, the blockhouse service, except for keeping the materiel in repair, was reduced to almost nothing more than maintaining a permanent watch. Grange played the role of a janitor, his empty concrete block visited every now and then by some official commission that scowled because the embrasures were not yet fitted with their regulation *funnels*, unceremoniously replaced for the moment by sandbags (when he took them into the block, keys in his hand, Grange acted almost contrite: he felt the reproving, somewhat disgusted stare of the Engineers' officers upon him, eying him as if he were a hobo filling his broken windowframes with newspaper; he always felt obliged to lead them out with a vaguely apologetic gesture toward the vaulting, as if to say something like: "The walls are good!").

In good weather, he often went down to the hamlet of Les Falizes for the afternoon. Half a mile from the blockhouse, the tiny white road came to an end in a fresh upland meadow where a dozen cottages basked in the solitude of high stubble and the encircling firs. Grange turned left at the Bihoreau farm, a rest home whose shutters were closed now, and sat down at the

Cafe des Platanes, which lodged whatever improbable guests might appear out of this wilderness. In front of the one-story house, on a tidy little paved terrace overlooking the road, were a table, two red-and-white-striped iron chairs, and even—a surprising touch of modernity—an orange parasol folded around its pole; not long past noon, the shadow of a huge chestnut tree fell across the terrace. After exchanging a few compliments with Madame Tranet, who appeared, smiling, behind her curtain of glass beads like a figurine on a barometer ("here's my lieutenant back with the good weather"), and commiserating with her on the war's uncertainties and the demands of rationing, Grange installed himself in his garden chair, sipped his coffee, and plunged into a kind of dreamy beatitude. At this time of the afternoon, the village was usually quite empty; the houses scattered across the meadow, the black-and-white cows grazing here and there in the clearing, the yellower sun of the last autumn days, the rest home with its closed shutters—everything reminded him of the sweetness of high mountain meadows, of the season when the herds gather and the little summer hotels, the last tourist gone, close well ahead of the first snow. Behind this timid and still golden beauty, this snug, late-season peace, he could feel the cold rising, reaching across the land, a cutting chill that was not winter's: the clearing was like an island in the vague intimidation that seemed to rise from these black woods. "That's it. I'm the season's last summer visitor: it's over," Grange thought, with a shrinking feeling around his heart, looking at the freshly painted table, the parasol, the chestnut tree, the sunny meadow. "Ten years of childhood in vacationland: the years of fat cows. Now it's done with." When he closed his eyes, he could hear only two faint sounds: the cracked bells of the little black cows harnessed in pairs to make it easy finding them when they wandered off into the woods, and another sound that seemed to rise out of the depths of his past: the *recitation* of some ten children in the tiny school-house down the road that must have been a blacksmith shop once. He felt something like a tide rising in him at that, something inert and despairing which was close to the brink of tears.

As soon as the sun started sinking, the villagers emerged one by one from the edge of the woods and came home along the road with their carts and bundles of firewood: chopping down trees and raising piebald cows seemed to be their only occupation. As they passed beneath the chestnut tree they greeted Grange with weather-wise observations—there was never any mention of the war—and sometimes the Bihoreau boy would have a drink with him, though it was up to Grange to make conversation. His melancholy soon passed, and he began to feel almost important here: it was as if he were some good-natured *vidame* coming down from his castle keep to enjoy the evening's cool with the peasants of his manor.

When he returned before nightfall, he rarely failed to climb down into the concrete block for a brief inspection; this was what he called "keeping an eye on the blockhouse." As a matter of fact, there was no need for an eye there—the concrete cell remained locked up all day long—but Grange had developed a strange compulsion: he liked to stay inside it for a few minutes at sundown. In good moods, he mocked himself about it: wasn't he like those ship's engineers too long in the service who preferred smoking down in the hold? When he had closed the vault's heavy door behind him, he stood on the threshold for a moment, glanced around the walls and up at the low ceiling, never without apprehension: he was assailed by a sudden sense of being out of his element, at a loss. It was the room's diminunitiveness that first affected him: it was hard to co-ordinate what he saw with the structure's over-all dimensions; the feeling of confinement became oppressive: his body moved here like the dry kernel inside a nutshell. Then came the vivid sensation—Grange marveled how expressive the word was—of the hermetic *block* sealed around him—a sensation produced by the musty coolness that fell on his shoulders, the stale, aseptic dryness of the air, the tiny drops of concrete spattering the framework that articulated the redoubt in delicate ribs, sealing the floor to the walls, the walls to the ceiling. "A concrete dice-block," Grange mused, tapping the wall unconsciously—"a crate that might topple over: someone ought to paste on labels reading *top* and *bottom*—let's hope *fragile* will be unnecessary."

The room was bare, crude, with something violently

uninhabitable about it. In a far corner, the hatchway that opened into the escape tunnel was half covered by a mattress hung against the wall. To the left were piled munitions boxes and machine-gun belts—oilcans, jars of grease, and filthy rags made greenish blurs which looked like the smears on garage floors. To the right a red fire extinguisher and a white-enameled first-aid box with a red cross on it were attached to the wall. The middle of the room was empty; there was no place to stand in preference to any other; mechanically, Grange took a few steps toward the brutal shaft of light that cut through the gloom and stretched out for a second or two in the gun-layer's position beside the anti-tank gun. Through the narrow embrasure he saw only the road rising gently toward the horizon—constricted by the forest walls —the harsh color of broken slag, with a line of sugar-white, crystalline gravel on each side. Five hundred yards away, the road sank down behind a rise in the terrain; its flat bed and the double palisade of trees formed a battlement so sharply etched that its edges seemed silvered against the empty sky. Putting an eye to the sight, Grange could readily distinguish each twig along the battlement's edge, each sharp pebble in the road, and even the thin, shallow tracks the wheels had made. Unthinkingly he turned the aiming screw: slowly the sight-wires' slender black cross came to rest on the center of the battlement, a little above the road's surface at the horizon. In the curve of the crescent that brought together the vague white sky and the empty road, the least twig's motionlessness became fascinating: the great round eye with its two crossed hairs seemed to open on another world, silent, intimidating, and bathed in a white light, a soundless evidence. Grange realized he had been holding his breath for a moment and quickly stood up, shrugging his shoulders.

"Stupid!" he mumbled—but he noticed his hand was trembling.

At Les Falizes dinner was served early: for Grange this was always an agreeable moment. They sat down, all four together, around the little deal table Grange worked at during the day and which they dragged into the common room for dinner. Gourcuff usually fell asleep before the meal's end, but Hervouët, Olivon, and Grange often sat talking long afterwards near the stove, where a pot of harsh yet tasteless coffee was always steaming, as on the stoves of Flemish farms: "this is where the penates of Les Falizes are," Grange thought, when Olivon set down the cups and uncovered the pot with a ritual gesture; he was surprised at having found a hearth and home for himself so effortlessly.

The conversation flowed easily: Olivon, who had been a foreman in the shipyards of Penhoët, had friends in common with Hervouët, since half the men of La Brière worked in Saint-Nazaire. Both men were *leftists* and political discussions ran high: the strikes of '36, the Popular Front, rolled through the little room with the sound of the Grande Armée in the memories of soldiers on half pay; it was as if the war were only a *technical incident,* as they said on the radio, a curtain accidentally dropped by a remote stagehand at the play's most exciting moment. Then Hervouët would tell stories of his hunting adventures, of nights spent lying in wait while an image of the old singing, lascivious, poaching Briéron flickered before them, a kind of legendary hero who amused Grange because of his resemblance to Father Ierochka in *The Cossacks*. Sometimes, when the talk had lasted late, they listened to the broadcasts of the *Stuttgart Traitor*, who had once mentioned their regiment. After a long sputtering, all the war's unreality melted through the static into this thin, piercing voice, which lingered over its words, hissing like the villain of a melodrama. In the silences, they heard the branches dripping around the blockhouse, and sometimes, quite near, the sound of some large animal digging in the woods, which sent Hervouët running to look outside. Through the open window came a long, sumptuous rustle that seemed to dissolve into the breathing forest and the cry of the screech owls perched on the barbed wire, lured by the rodents that came to eat the rotten bread. The men were at ease together, good-humored and relaxed in the comforting warmth, only a little disquieted by this murmur from the wild, this window open to the troublesome darkness. It was the moment Gourcuff always chose to wake up: the jokes that greeted his childish yawns were the signal for going to bed.

"A hell of a war!" Olivon remarked, stretching as he filled the empty pot. The men said good night and went back to their quarters, which over-looked the barb-wire emplacement; Grange called it the crew room. Leaning out, he noticed the sudden glow of Hervouët's cigarette at the next window—before leaving to set his traps, the soldier was sniffing the wet woods like a hound.

Back in his own room, Grange read for a few moments by the weak light of a lantern, but too many cups of coffee after dinner set his nerves on edge, and if the weather was dry and there was a moon, he took a short walk before going to bed. The forest night was never completely dark. In the direction of the distant Meuse, the opposite slope, in the gaps between the trees, whitened vaguely with a sort of momentary false dawn, a silky palpitation of soft, sluggish flashes, like the great bubbles of light that regularly burst over valleys of blast furnaces: these gleams were the concrete casemates being constructed on accelerated schedules, poured at night under arc lights. Toward the frontier, where the plateau rose to meet the horizon, he could see tiny beads of light forming one by one and sliding for a few seconds down the night, noiselessly broadening and sweeping the tree-tops with a sudden beam: the Belgian automobiles driving toward the peace of another world, flashing across the wider clearings where the Ardennes gradually petered out.

Between these two fringes which suddenly disturbed the night in this vague fashion, the Roof (this was Grange's name for the high forest plateau hung above the valley) remained plunged in profound darkness. The road stretched out as far as the eye could reach like a phantom path, its powdering of white gravel half-phosphorescent between the trees. The air was soft and warm, heavy with the smell of plants; it was good to walk on this loud, crunching path, hidden by the shadow of the branches, with over his head this streak of paler sky that was somehow alive, occasionally wakening to the reflection of distant lights. Grange walked on, his sense of physical well-being marred by troubled thoughts: the night protected him, gave him this easy breathing and this prowler's freedom of movement, but it was the night that brought the war closer: as if a fiery sword were writing great pure characters above the world that cowered in primordial fear; roused, the sky over the woods watched dark France, dark Germany, and between the two the strange, calm scintillation of Belgium, whose lights died away at the horizon's edge. The night was not sleeping; he felt as if the vigilant earth had assumed the darkness like a camouflage; his eyes automatically followed the searchlights' distant pencils that intersected now and then, seeming to grope their way through the air, cautious as insect antennae behind the vast and disquieting horizon.

Grange left the road, turning off on a service path toward Hill 457, a sharp rise of ground recently cleared, from which a view extended far across the plateau; he sat down on a stump, lit a cigarette, and stared for a long time into the night torn by sudden flashes and gleams. From here the glowworms suddenly became more numerous, forming against the horizon almost a half-circle of sudden winks that seemed to warn, to wonder; they were like a populous coast seen from the open sea on a clear night: he felt as if a question it had become urgent to understand were being asked—but Grange did not understand: he merely felt a certain feverishness rising within him after a little while, and around his eyes the faint constrictions of insomnia; he wanted to walk in this overwakeful night until exhaustion came, until morning.

By the time he returned to the road, everything was calm again: the night breathed gently in the shadow of the trees; noiselessly he climbed the stairs to the house. Before going to bed he stood for a moment in front of the crew-room door which the men left open at night to catch the stove's last warmth; out of the darkness came the sound of heavy, healthy breathing that made him smile in spite of himself: the world around him was troubled and uncertain, but there was this sleep as well. "All four," he thought as he closed the door, and felt something like a desire to whistle. He was amazed to realize that two weeks before he hadn't even known their names.

OFTEN, on Sundays, Captain Varin, who was in command of the company, invited Grange to lunch at Moriarmé. Sometimes the lieutenant rode down in the provisions truck; but on clear days, rather than borrow a bicycle from Les Falizes and be jolted for seven miles down the torrential bed of rough gravel, he preferred to walk; besides, he was grateful for this bad road which left him a free hand and virtually cut off the Roof from the inhabited world.

He started out early; as he approached l'Eclaterie, he listened for the sound of Moriarmé's bells rising from the valley after High Mass: their high-pitched chime fading into the great circle of the woods pleased him like a half-forgotten sign of welcome: it was a sound that never reached the silent Roof.

He found the officers of both companies—the 1st and 3rd took their mess together—already started on their *apéritifs;* from one window he could see the Meuse, a deep oily color at the foot of its overhanging forests, and from the other the church square where civilians in Sunday clothes were already lining up in front of the pastryshop. Around the table reigned a noisy and virtually continuous cordiality: it was evident that Captain Varin's Sundays, which now and then collected the *rangers* scattered in the wilderness blockhouses, had something to do with the maintenance of *esprit de corps.*

Grange soon saw what kind of man was in command of the 3rd Company: Captain Magnard was a petulant blond—perhaps too consciously handsome—with the tender blue eyes of a womanizer, as carefully groomed as if he were wearing a corset, like officers during the Dreyfus Affair, and with the capricious condescension of a *chasseur* transferred to a camp behind the lines; he published occasional patriotic verses in *l'Echo du Front,* the corps paper circulated by the Army, and if asked once or twice, he would start reciting over the dessert. Grange supposed that the day war was declared the man had assumed his old-campaigner's tone the way he might put a flower in his buttonhole the morning of *the happiest day of his life*—the marriage had not been consummated, and the flower looked dead to all eyes but his own. "A ribbon clerk who's just left his whore's bed,"

Grange decided, supremely irritated when the man minutely described some village conquest in his crude terms.

Captain Varin was distant and rather unconcerned, but occasionally his eyes unhooded themselves behind his wineglass and glowed for a second like the bulb in a target when some particular oafishness roused him; evidently he was having to bear with the luncheon, and with Magnard more than all the rest. "As for us, he doesn't miss a thing, he keeps track," Grange told himself, a little stung, but deciding that the restraint Varin imposed on the meal was not unpleasant: it was like the curé's presence at a wedding breakfast, it warded off the worst. The conversation was of a pitiful simplicity; the humor that of a compartment full of traveling salesmen; after glasses had been clinked and a few choruses brayed, there were several moments of silence when the high spirits evaporated. Captain Magnard patronized the reservists and the young officers with a comic broadness; it was by slaps on the shoulder and clay pipes pushed familiarly under their noses that he "gave them confidence."

"At the colonel's? You'll get a queer name for yourself, if you don't watch out, fellow," his nasal drawl suddenly cut through the other voices, with a familiarity all too recently assumed. There was a lot of drinking. "Every man here is worth more than he looks, Grange thought, exasperated: "the paterfamilias at the brothel." Outside the window, the Meuse slowly darkened, dimmed by the cliff shadow; the vacant boredom of a provincial Sunday leaked through the casements despite the war; the air smelled of pernod, stale cigar smoke, and heavy food. Obviously something was being simulated here, but what? In the moments of silence, the guests looked out the window at the catechism class lining up in the square for vespers.

"That's enough about the service!" drawled Captain Magnard's affected, slightly drunk voice. *"Had any ass lately?"*

Sometimes, after lunch, Grange accompanied a fellow officer through the dozing Sunday streets to the Charleville train, then stopped at the Company office to settle some service details. Captain Varin was always there, smoking his cigarette behind stacks of papers. His face was heavy and somewhat carnivorous-looking, the hard mustache still black, the raked nostril flaring, the jaw massive; at first glance, he seemed only a rather heavily turned-out old trooper, but a trooper who never drank, never joked, never even laughed, and, since the division had been in the sector, never once set foot in the Charleville whorehouse the other officers took turns visiting on Sundays. He commanded his company with icy competence, holding men and officers alike on short rein, announced his decisions briefly, his voice harsh, listened attentively, and never argued. He was born to the "I give orders or I keep still" manner—he must have chosen the wrong war or else the wrong army, Grange thought (the captain intrigued him)—always astonished by this bare office where everything breathed regulations, as harshly scrubbed as a convent parlor, with no chair for a visitor, not even a bottle of *apéritif*. Yet on Sundays there was something else. Alone with the captain, Grange occasionally, for a few seconds, felt him come closer, almost to the point of openness—not that he relaxed: he worked all day long; not that he became more human: his confidence was impersonal to the point of coldness— Varin's attitude had nothing to do with putting Grange at ease. The captain spoke of the war. Grange decided that Varin talked about it with him because he, too, had never asked leave for Charleville, which caused talk— and perhaps because he was still young: the captain's secret vice was to scandalize his colleagues.

"Look at this for a minute, Grange. The Second Office is spoiling us."

The document, to which was clipped a red card reading "To be communicated only to the officers' units," was a complete series of photographs showing the different kinds of casemates in the Siegfried line. Most were in forest emplacements, like Les Falizes—the angle of the excellent shots revealed the dark embrasures with their paler circular flanges. The whole thing, consisting of loose-leaf sheets of glossy paper in a ringed notebook, with measurements of the structures and reference numbers, reminded him of the careful presentation of spring collections at a tailor's shop.

"Which does Monsieur prefer—this one, or perhaps this?" The captain grimaced slightly; it was evident that the glossy paper in particular aroused his sovereign antipathy; he was probably thinking that the general-staff puppies were putting on airs. . . . "Pretty, aren't they?"

He winked, rubbing his finger over the shiny paper, indicating a heavy model that had three embrasures and looked rather unwieldy beneath the overhanging pines.

"Pretty or not, in any case, I advise you to get them into your head, lieutenant."

"Because . . . we're going to attack?"

"Because neither you nor I will ever see these music boxes any closer than this. You know what this means?" The captain began walking up and down, spurred by a cunning daemon. "It's an old trick. GHQ sends us its travel souvenirs with postmarks attached. There are bridegrooms like that—they invent a honeymoon for the audience. It makes you more important with your friends, or the boys at the office. I suppose the Poles found this reassuring."

"The Germans aren't moving either," hazarded Grange, always exhilarated by this pessimistic strategy: he liked encouraging people to follow their inclinations. "Perhaps they'll never attack."

The captain fixed him with his leaden look. His nostrils quivered. "It's strange," Grange thought. "He doesn't even see me. He's shooting down an objection. He may not be an intellectual, but at least he can keep an idea in his head with a certain amount of irony."

"Then what are you waiting for here, young fellow —post cards?"

"Here?"

" 'Here'? . . ." The captain gave a worn, rather sinister laugh. " 'Here'? What do you mean 'here'? *Here* just the same as anywhere else. And it'll be a kind of lark, won't it . . . a stroll with a cane in your hand!"

After these sudden outbursts, the captain dismissed him rather dryly and plunged back into his papers: there was no use trying to strike fire again for another week. Grange emerged from these consultations half diverted, half disturbed. It was like a bloodletting: it relieved you, he told himself; however strange he found it—for he himself followed the war's progress with great indifference—Grange understood that the captain was suffering. When he was outside in the street again, it seemed as if the light had faded; a great dark crescent cast by the cliff was already gnawing at the other bank of the Meuse. He decided he had nothing else to do in these blank, empty streets where bicycles were piled in front of the cafes and a few soldiers, already drunk, were staggering toward the railway station: he was eager to get back to the shelter of his woods. The captain's remarks were spoiling his day; not that he believed them, but they landed in the silent, muffled life Grange had created for himself like a stone thrown into a pond that had seemed so inviting beneath its watery lens: in a second you saw how black the water was, and your nostrils filled with an obstinate rotten odor you couldn't forget again. "The war? he wondered, shrugging his shoulders peevishly, "who knows if there even is a war? If there were, we'd hear about it."

But his nerves bothered him nevertheless; he thought about this army dozing around him like a man napping on the grass who even in his sleep turns and brushes away the wasp buzzing about his head. Walking along the river bank, the lieutenant glanced—already suspiciously —at the little blockhouses whose embrasures surveyed the Meuse at long intervals: he found them paltry, shabby, their concrete substructure and brick tops looking as if they had begun as casemates and ended up as provincial bus stations. Of course, this isn't the Maginot Line, Grange thought, raising his eyes unconsciously towards the bushy eagles' nests that bristled high over the river —in fact this indolent fortification was somehow re-assuring: obviously nothing serious was expected here. Behind these forests . . .

And then the winter was coming: in a few weeks there would be snow. There would be days when the truck wouldn't come up any more: with a thrill of pleasure Grange contemplated the prospect of being im-prisoned at Les Falizes, cloistered in his mountain retreat around the red-hot stove, snowbound for long days in the fairy-tale forest. In April, the Ardennes slope was still white with snow while the valley apple trees were in bloom. . . .

"Varin's angry because they've stuck him here on this make-believe front: everyone in the regular army wants promotion." As soon as the road's zigzags penetrated the forest, he felt himself breathing more easily; at each turn he saw Moriarmé shrinking back into the valley. Grange walked on in the moist silence that closed over him: he felt light, young again: merely vanishing into this forest that surrounded him as far as the eye could reach revived a sense of well-being that swelled his lungs. The air smelled as it does after a shower: before nightfall, it would rain on the Roof; at Les Falizes, the world was different. Then suddenly, at a turn in the road, the sting returned, the pinprick that made him frown.

"Then what are you waiting for here, young fellow—post cards?"

One day when he was climbing up to the blockhouse this way—it was one of the last Sundays in November—the rain surprised Grange at the first turn, and he had scarcely reached the plateau when it became a regular downpour. The light was already fading from the sky, and the clouds rolled along the edge of the Roof, clinging occasionally to the rises of the plateau which then vanished, wrapped in the lingering mist: this was the herald of one of those long rains that wrung out the soft clouds for whole days over the Roof. Whenever the rain settled in like this, Grange felt alert and good-humored; the sharper sense that he was on his way home flowed through his limbs like a warm draught: already he saw *his men* sitting around the stove in the common-room where the wet overcoats were steaming on their hooks. He walked on through the downpour at a steady pace, conscious only of a slight fatigue, his left hand holding his sopping coat collar away from his chin and the cold drops sliding down his neck one by one.

Glancing down a service path, he saw that a cottony fog walled him in twenty feet away; he advanced in a clearing of the fog which moved as he moved—only the road before him, where the branches held the fog off the ground, showed paler in the gloom. This stretch through the fogbound forest gradually lulled Grange into his favorite daydream; in it he saw an image of his life: all that he had, he carried with him; twenty feet away, the world grew dark, perspectives blurred, and there was nothing near him but this close halo of warm consciousness, this nest perched high above the vague earth.

On the plateau, where the roadbed drained badly, puddles stretched across the pebbly surface, puckered by the raindrops' bouncing gray bubbles. When he raised his eyes to the horizon, he noticed a figure some distance ahead of him splashing from puddle to puddle, still nebulous in the curtain of rain. In silhouette it looked like a little girl wearing a long, hooded cloak much too big for her and knee-high rubber boots; watching her pick her way along the uneven road, her back a little bent, as if she were lugging a leather satchel over her shoulder, he first thought it was a schoolgirl on her way home, though he knew there were no houses for at least two miles, and suddenly he remembered that it was Sunday; he began observing the diminutive figure more attentively. There was something that intrigued him in her way of walking; beneath the continuous patter of the downpour, to which she seemed quite oblivious, she certainly looked like a child playing truant. Sometimes she would jump over a puddle, feet together, sometimes she would stop beside the road and break off a branch—once she half turned round and seemed to glance behind her, as if to measure how much nearer Grange had come, then started hopping on one foot, kicking a pebble in front of her, ran a few steps, making the puddles dance—and once or twice, in spite of the distance, Grange even thought he could hear her whistling. The road grew lonelier still, the enveloping downpour making the forest rustle from one end to the other.

"She must be a rain-sprite," Grange thought, smiling unconsciously behind his streaming collar, "a naiad—a little forest witch." He began to slow down despite the rain; he didn't want to catch up with her too quickly— he was afraid the sound of his steps might alarm the girl, keep her from her graceful, solitary wild-creature's games. Now that he had come a little nearer, she was no longer quite a little girl: when she ran a few steps, her hips were almost a woman's; her childlike, playful neck movements were those of a runaway colt, but every now and then appeared a provocative curve that suddenly suggested something quite different, as if her head remembered of its own accord having rested on a man's shoulder. Grange wondered, a trifle annoyed, if she had really noticed he was walking behind her: sometimes she stopped beside the road and gave a happy laugh, as you might address a friend roped behind you on a mountain-climbing expedition; then, for minutes at a time, she seemed to have forgotten him, resuming her romping, tomboy gait—and suddenly she seemed utterly alone, *about her own business*, like a kitten that ignores you for a ball of string. They went on this way for a moment. Despite the noise of the rain, the road's pale trough seemed to Grange to run through a clearing: he was merely a man walking behind a woman, all pounding blood and violent curiosity. "A little girl!" he told himself uneasily—but unconsciously his heart beat faster each time the silhouette stopped at the roadside and a hand half opened the long cape's hood for a moment. Suddenly the figure planted itself in the middle of the road and, standing in a puddle that reached to her ankles, the girl began washing the sides of her rubber boots in the water; when he reached her, Grange discovered under the hood tilted in his direction two bright blue eyes as sharp and warm as a spring thaw—and, deep inside, as if in a crib, the soft straw of her yellow hair.

"You keep your woods p-pretty wet, don't you?" asked a fresh, abrupt little voice, while the person in the cloak shook herself with puppyish unconcern, showering Grange—then all at once the chin rose gently, tenderly holding up the face to the rain as if for a kiss, the eyes dancing.

"Let's walk together," she continued, in a voice that admitted no contradiction. "It's more fun."

She began laughing again—her fresh, rainy laugh. Now that he had caught up with her, she walked beside him at a good speed. From time to time Grange glanced at her surreptitiously; around the edge of the hood he could see only her glistening nose and mouth and the short chin set against the rain, but he was stirred to feel her near him, young and vital, supple as a fawn in the warm scent of wet wool. She had fallen in step with him of her own accord: it was as if she had taken his arm. Sometimes she turned her head slightly and the dark hood's edge revealed eyes the color of a brightening sky; whenever their eyes met they laughed a little without speaking, a laugh of pure delight. She had thrust her hands deep into the pockets of her cloak with the simple gesture of a farm girl afraid of frostbite. "But she's not a country girl," Grange decided, his heart leaping, "and she's not really a girl at all. How old is she? Where is she going?" Merely walking beside her was so delightful he dared not question her: he was afraid of breaking the spell.

"I was waiting for you back there on the hill. You didn't walk fast then!" she said suddenly, tossing her offended head and at the same time glancing at him obliquely. There was a kind of conscious mockery in her voice that exposed Grange's stratagem. The tone of voice indicated that she hadn't been deceived about such things for a long time. She was quite aware how attractive she was.

"I wanted an escort," she added quickly, apparently repeating a lesson not quite understood. "Sunday nights, there are often soldiers on the road. They say they *mis*behave themselves," she added, gravely nodding her head again—but he felt that she wasn't very frightened.

"And you weren't afraid of me?"

"Oh, I know you!"

She skipped ahead down the road: life seemed released in this graceful body like a colt in a meadow.

". . . I've seen you from my house. Every day you come to Les Platanes for coffee. . . . It's *ostentatious!*" she added, emphasizing the word with a meaningful look, as if she had just learned it—but again the chin held up her mouth to him and her eyes danced, while her neck curved in a way Grange found disturbing. At each word, at each movement of her head and shoulders, his notion of her changed decisively.

They walked on again in silence for a moment. The rain was not so heavy now, but fell straight down, good for several hours. The wind had dropped and the light was beginning to fade: the mist-choked woods around them dripped heavily.

"And you're—you're vacationing here?" Grange asked suddenly, quite Machiavellian. Yes, that was it— she must be a schoolgirl. And he remembered she had said "your woods."

"Oh no! . . . I'm a widow!" she said after a moment, in a reasonable little voice that was quite sure of itself. "I have a *family ration book!*" she continued with childish glee; rummaging in the inside pocket of her cape, she pulled out a yellowish booklet with an official seal and dog-eared pages. Grange, startled, blinked for a moment: every second he felt a new gust of wind take his breath away.

"It's very sad!" she concluded, nodding with comic gravity, like a little girl playing "visits." And then, standing in the rain in the middle of the road, they both burst into helpless laughter.

Through her disconnected sentences, Grange began to see her situation a little less fancifully. Early in the year she had married a young doctor who, probably dazzled by her beauty, had carried her off from her classrooms without a moment's hesitation: two months later he had left her a widow. At least that must be what her sudden confidences meant him to infer, for in her account the doctor appeared only as "Jacquot," which seemed to be a sufficient identification for him. After his death, her father—who passed in her remarks for a remote and rather absent-minded providence—had rented a house for her at Les Falizes. "Jacquot," before abandoning her so suddenly, had been worried about her because of a shadow on one lung, which seemed to have assumed for her afterwards the purely poetic significance of a deathbed wish rather than a disease. She had come up here to cure herself, or rather to obey his last request, in the forest, where the war had found her like a bird on a branch. She had stayed on.

"It's good for you!" she declared, energetically shaking her head, which looked quite tiny inside the hood.

Grange listened to her, but such details remained peculiarly vague for him. The words "father" and "husband" had no hold over her; they rested on her for a moment like a garment put on and taken off, but did not involve her. Wherever she was, you felt, she was complete. How dense, how concrete the present became, in her shadow. With what force of conviction, with what energy she was *here!* She had taken his arm to cross a puddle and kept it now; he felt the grip of her light fingers through his coat; her skin glistening in the rain, her step firm, she was anything but unsubstantial; suddenly she leaned against him, as round and perfect as a pebble on the road.

"You must take me home," she said, when they reached the path. "It's *gallant.* Julia will make us tea (more riddles, Grange thought, vexed by the appearance of another character on the scene). I'm always so frightened in the big oaks!"

When they took the narrow path to Les Falizes, night suddenly seemed to fall with the shadow of the great trees. The rain had stopped for a moment: turning to look down the road toward the Meuse where the sky was clearing, they saw a streak of dull red disappearing on the horizon, the same western glow that fades on snowy nights. Here the path entered a grove of high trees; the night's chill fell on their shoulders from a thick dome of wet branches. Grange noticed she was shivering and pressed his arm around her without speaking: suddenly his gaiety vanished and he was overcome by a grave, tender pity: it was dark now, and here was this defenseless girl beside him, lost in the war's forest: he wanted to speak her name.

"My name is Mona," she said, her voice a little hoarse.

He saw her head bending and suddenly felt her lips on the back of his hand. "I like you," she added suddenly, with a rather ambiguous gentleness, and once again Grange felt disturbed, uncertain. She was spontaneous, but she was not clear: like spring freshets full of earth and leaves. Her words were a child's, but their boldness was not at all naïve; there, suddenly, on his hand, was a fleshy mouth with lips that already knew how to find what they wanted.

When they came out of the woods, night had already extinguished the village in the clearing; only one square of light shone from the open door of Les Platanes onto the little terrace, disengaging the low branches of the chestnut tree from the darkness; then, faintly at first, the cluster of low cottages appeared around them in the grass, their roofs barely showing above the garden fences. Grange had never come to Les Falizes at night: here, they were suddenly very far away; lying at full length upon the ground, a forgotten life paused in the clearing and drew its quiet breath, immersed up to its nostrils in the odor of plants, the creeping emanations of wet earth. Mona released his arm, and, running ahead on the path, began to shout toward one of the dark houses at the top of her lungs, using her hands as a megaphone.

"Julia! Tea! Bring tea, my love, lots of tea, darling! We have company. . . . An officer. A *handsome* officer! . . ." A few seconds later a little bell rang wildly behind the hedge, a gate creaked, doors slammed, rousing the clearing's echoes with a housewifely din.

The rather large room Grange stepped into gave an impression of comfortable warmth and almost of luxury, surprising in this forgotten village after the muddy billets of the Meuse. To judge from the heavy rafters, the great, rough chimney with its slate hearthstone, the peasant-style double door with its leaves opening one above the other and its wrought-iron bolts and latches, this was an old farm that had been remodeled for summer visitors or for the boar hunters who came up here in the fall. The floor was covered with a thick carpet; the light from a raffia-shaded lamp and the bramble fire crackling on the hearth drew several pieces of heavily-waxed, pot-bellied country furniture out of the shadows. In one corner he could see a day bed, and above it shelves stuffed with books; in the middle of the room stood a low Moroccan table made out of a great embossed brass tray. It was evident that the taste in charge of this refurnishing was strict in its own way, even severe; yet over these massive pieces, this foursquare arrangement, was cast the charming disorder of a nursery. Records in torn covers and open books lay piled on the carpet, glass marbles rolled behind the armchair cushions, salacious post cards were thumbtacked to the walls with pictures of actors and newspaper clippings. On a cord stretched from the cupboard keyhole to the window latch hung various articles of feminine underwear—a heavy stable lantern was suspended over the bed by a complicated system of string and clothespins. Between the two wrought-iron brackets in the corner opposite the bed was slung a hammock, in which lay a litter of fashion magazines, a harmonica, a pair of read leather slippers, nail scissors, a fan, and a huge, carved Spanish tortoise-shell comb. Above this gypsy-camp disorder floated a faint stimulating odor, a morning scent—more distinctly than on the road, Grange smelled the forest around him here.

As soon as they were inside, Mona had wriggled out of her cloak, which flew across the room and landed on the clothesline. A flood of wheat-colored hair fell down her shoulders, reaching to the small of her back. Beneath her cloak she was wearing a blue, ink-stained blouse and a skirt. Her neck, once she had let down the burden of her hair, assumed a more languid bend, and when she shifted her shoulders a little to caress them with this heavy curtain of hair, she was entirely a woman again, as warm as an unmade bed.

"Come and warm yourself," she said, taking his hand and drawing him before the crackling thorns with boyish brusqueness, but the "*tu*" did not surprise Grange at all: it was obvious that in her speech "*vous*" was more unaccustomed and strained. "Say hello to Julia —she takes care of me," and, turning around, he discovered a pair of inquisitive, circumspect eyes staring at him behind the tea tray, a maid as childish-looking as Mona, whose manners she evidently imitated, save that she wore her hair short and curly and used lipstick. Tied around her waist was a white lace apron so small that it seemed purely emblematic, but in Julia, who had only the natural beauty of her youth, the somewhat disturbing quality of Mona's looks turned to downright suggestiveness: despite the innocence of her eyes, Julia's mascara and lipstick, her small, bold breasts, and the tiny excuse for an apron gave her the air of a soubrette in a magazine for men.

"Let me fix your hair, dear," Mona said, handing Grange her cup, throwing her arm around Julia's neck, and pulling her in front of the mirror. Her mouth full of hairpins, she rummaged among Julia's curls, the girl laughing beneath her tickling fingers and swaying her hips a little as she glanced over her shoulder at Grange. Amid too-shrill laughter, a sudden red flare from the hearth revealed two laughing witches somehow at liberty in the chaotic houschold of a sorcerer's apprentice.

When Julia had disappeared with the tea tray, there were several moments' silence. Outside the half-open window, behind the closed shutters with their heart-shaped perforations, Grange heard the forest dripping, and sometimes, quite close, the creak of branches rising again after the downpour. Mona sat on the edge of the divan, heaving a little sigh of fatigue, and then, with that thrust of her chin already familiar, once again threw back her hair and lifted her eyes and her mouth to Grange, with the movement of a plant turning to the sun.

"Take off my boots for me," she said in a low, almost hoarse voice. "My feet are so cold—they're all wet."

Under her rubber boots, each with a puddle of water

inside, she wore heavy men's wool socks, now completely soaked. Grange slipped them off. His eyes were smarting, a painful tenderness filled his throat, and he realized he was clenching his teeth to keep them from chattering. He touched the wet toes curling under with cold, then the smooth sole: a few shreds of wool had caught at the edge of the slightly bluish toenails; suddenly an overwhelming sense of pity flooded through him: he pressed his mouth against the icy toes until he felt the wool against his teeth.

Suddenly Mona wrenched her body backward with the furious thrust of a trapped animal, and, throwing herself flat on the day bed, pulled him against her with both hands; he felt his mouth upon hers, and her entire woman's body against him, heavy and full, open as the furrowed earth. In a matter of seconds she was naked, her clothes torn off by a violent storm that pasted them against the furniture like washing blown into a thorn bush, but at the cyclone's center was this mouth that clung to his own so frankly, so greedily; he discovered he was within her without knowing when it had happened. "You're a paradise!" he gasped with a kind of calm stupefaction; and he was astonished at his own words. When her finger tips had groped toward the lamp and put it out, the room seemed plunged in a pool of dim water; only the transom over the door and the heart-shaped holes in the shutters made pale spots in the darkness; the woods had stopped dripping, the moon must have risen over the forest; he took her again, gently, and from the soles of her feet to the roots of her hair she trembled—not feverishly, but almost solemnly, like a young tree answering the wind with all its leaves. He felt neither strain nor anxiety: as if a river murmured in the shade of trees, at noon. "Like a fish in its stream," he thought. "I've found my element; it's easy, I can always be happy here." From time to time, he took between his lips first one and then the other nipple of her breasts, which slipped a little to each side of her chest: he felt the long nocturnal thrust from deep within her that raised them again his lips.

"How good you are!" he told her in that undeceitful language he was beginning to discover, in which "good" no longer had any other meaning in the mind but 'good to take.'

"I have se*duced* you!" she whispered in a tiny, complacent voice, taking his head between her hands and pulling it a little away from hers to look at him with both eyes; then she pushed her headstrong mouth against his once more, and went on browsing. . . .

He walked back to the blockhouse in a cloud; when he wakened the next morning, bright sunshine was already moving across the room; even in his sleep he had heard the tiny, clear voice, already familiar as the fountain heard all night in the garden, parleying under his window with Olivon; he jumped out of bed and ran to the window, looking down at the blue hood planted there beneath his shutters as matter-of-fact as any mushroom.

"How wonderful!" he thought, blinking in the raw light—"it's starting again!" A moment afterwards, she was in his room: already the chin was lifting her fresh wet face to him; he looked at her, amazed, incredulous, as if she had come down the chimney.

THE cavalry's tanks and units of the mounted dragoons were maneuvering along the road. These were small units, for there was not enough room to spread out between the Meuse and the frontier, and the armored formations—if the rumors were to be believed—were being kept quite far behind the lines, in the Champagne camps; but the Meuse cavalry, in any case, was to operate in the Ardennes, strung out along these threadlike forest roads which the service paths connected so fragmentarily: apparently the essence of these exercises that sometimes awakened Les Falizes with the sudden roar of motors was to set the comb's teeth along the same line. On these days, when Olivon knocked early at Grange's door ("The *Tour de France* has started,

mon yeutenant"), the men left their hermitage and in
fine weather sat for hours beside the road, like woodsmen
of a manorial forest watching the great hunt processions
pass; furthermore, the cavalrymen they chatted with
during the halts, and who traveled far and fast in their
cars, constituted almost a port of call: they brought
news of friends who had vanished into the regular army
corps beyond the Meuse, a wind from abroad, a further
echo of the great world. Grange liked the cavalrymen:
officers and soldiers alike seemed younger to him than
the worn reservists he encountered at Moriarmé: an
eagerness circulated among them, like the atmosphere
that fills a stadium, a kind of swaggering that was not disagreeable—there was also a certain consolation, which he
did not try to explain too clearly to himself, in seeing
troops and materiel pass in good condition, destined to be
engaged far ahead of them the day the Germans attacked. The automatic machine guns, the half-tracks,
the dragoons' cars, paraded up the long slope toward
Belgium with the thunder of great herds of cattle, the
sound of the caterpillar treads on the rough gravel almost drowning out the whine of the motors in low gear.
Sometimes Grange would close his eyes and discover,
astonished, how the war, even in its most somnolent
moments, roused the ear so much more intimately than
the eye by this giant harrow's clatter passing over the
broken earth. He was struck too by the forest's facile
adaptation to these fierce and arrogant cavalcades. The
long perspectives of its roads, the tunnels running for

miles through the trees toward a mysterious disc of daylight at the horizon, were not made for the colorless lives of woodcutters and charcoal burners who had vegetated here waiting for the curtain to rise. The forest breathed, more ample now, awakened, alert, its remotest hiding places suddenly stirred by the enigmatic signs of time's reversion—an age of great hunts, of proud cavalcades—as if the old Merovingian lair were quickened by a forgotten scent in the air that made it live again.

Grange and Olivon were sitting not far from the road on empty gasoline tins, watching the armored units pass. They were not quite interested—the spectacle was hardly a new one—but they were not quite bored. Grange thought of the concierges straddling their kitchen chairs on summer evenings beside the boulevard traffic: in their way, Olivon and he were also escaping their airless porter's lodge: a free wind from far away passed over the road with these fast-moving troops.

Grange was fascinated by the tanks: he wondered what new kind of soul the lurching inhabitants of these heavy machines might unexpectedly develop: a fellow officer had spoken to him once of the strange, irrational security you felt, suddenly, just rolling along inside that way, your helmet lining pressed up against the armor plate in that colossal racket. Officers constantly doubled the column in their command cars along the road's shoulders; the convoy flowed on as far as the eye could reach in a grinding of gears, enveloped by a heavy cocoon of gray smoke that hung above the road, powdering every twig with a thick layer of grayish-brown flour that resembled the dust on a limekiln road. The machinery slid over the gravel like a river in spate, very dirty and very gray, with bottlenecks and eddies, a clatter of stones and a lashing of branches, almost as if it were a phenomenon of nature: Grange felt that the war had installed its furniture in the landscape with the —exhausting—casualness of those overprovided tenants who never see the end of the trunks they are expecting.

"It's just the same," Olivon remarked, shrugging his shoulders when he had watched the clattering procession for a long time without saying a word—"they don't have it any easier in the cavalry. That's no road to drag tanks over."

"There's not much chance of doing them any harm."

"Oh, that's not it, *mon yeutenant*." Olivon shrugged again. "It's the treads. They wear out. . . ."

Grange stared at him, nonplused. Olivon always staggered him. "There's no doubt about it," he thought, "you see everything in a war. Even soldiers trying to economize."

"See if you can find us something to drink," he said. He sensed that Olivon wanted to talk. It was one of those days when he *made up the war*, as Grange said: the passing cavalry always suggested his own notions of strategy. Grange handed him the key to the concrete block: they kept their bottles cool in the escape tunnel. Once they had glasses in their hands, each vehicle behind its dust cloud offered a salvo of heavy-handed jokes and thirsty noises as it passed. When Olivon occasionally toasted the convoy, holding the bottle at arm's length, the cries redoubled, as when Punch lifts the curtain.

"They're not thirsty," Grange decided grudgingly. "They're saluting a fetish."

"They'll do anything for it, *mon yeutanant*." Olivon shook his head with an aggrieved expression. "In this army, all they care about is drinking."

"What's the matter, Olivon?"

"Some days . . ." He shrugged his shoulders. "I'm not saying we don't have it easy. Sometimes I'd almost . . ." He shook the bottle over the gravel with an air of pretended indifference. "They talk big in the cavalry. They say if there's a heavy attack, they're supposed to fall back to Liège. It takes them four hours."

"Maybe."

Grange liked to discourage curiosity, his own first of all. Instinctively, he reacted to all war news—whatever snatches of information managed to reach him, rumors about the turn the campaign might take one day or the next—the way skin tautens and shrinks before a needle's point. These provinces of the phony war were habitable, even comfortable, provided you lived in them as if the air's oxygen content were lowered, as if the light had imperceptibly dimmed: it was a world where there was no longer any good news: you survived by ignoring all extremities, concealed by guilty stratagems that shifted with every wind, from minute to minute, at the thought of what might happen; a world, in fact, of diseases that were painless but annoyingly prone to take a turn for the worse—a world of *prognosis reserved.*

"There are farms, down at Les Falizes; the mayor went round there the day before yesterday. Told them to send their kids inland," Olivon continued. He always managed not to look at Grange, fixing his eyes on the road where the wheels were churning up the gravel as fast as they could go.

"There's been no evacuation order."

"No? . . ." Olivon weighed the news gravely, but did not seem completely reassured. "Even so, someone big went through Moriarmé yesterday. Hervouët heard about it at the yard."

"Someone big?"

"Yes, big: generals," Olivon said, with a bored grimace. "For inspection. Even went up to the border. Around the blockhouse at Les Buttés."

Grange was always surprised by this subtle network of intelligence that circulated among the men, carefully short-circuiting the officers as if they were settlers isolated among native hordes.

"Then we won't have them here, at least."

"That's for sure!" This time Olivon turned to Grange with a relieved, momentary smile. "All the same," he resumed, gloomy again, "it's a bad sign. They've been putting the heavy stuff behind the Meuse for eight days. It might be for this week. . . ."

"What do you mean 'it'?"

"Oh, well, *mon yeutenant . . .*" Olivon turned his head away with an embarrassment that was almost scandalized . . . "The big push, you know. . . ."

"*And the sun is unmentioned, but his power is among us,*" Grange thought. A prickling sensation ran between his neck and his shirt collar. His mind was so constituted that a logical idea of his own rarely unsettled it, but someone else's premonition penetrated there with almost no resistance: what had merely irritated him coming from Varin now attacked his nerves in a subtler fashion: it was like the smell of lightning in the air, the cattle's contagious fear before the storm.

"The Germans aren't crazy," he said, shrugging his shoulders. "In November! Once it's snowed, the roads around here . . ."

He prodded unenthusiastically with the end of his switch at the litter of dead leaves the wind had heaped beside the road. They fluttered a moment in the eddying wake of the tanks, already dry and gray. On each side of the road, between the naked branches, a paler sky now appeared over the diminished forest. Far away, against the shaggy surface of the trees, a slender coil of dust rose slowly above the branches: the cavalry was maneuvering on the road to Les Houches as well. The war was settling in, not steadily or fast, but by sudden, almost imperceptible touches taking possession of the earth, like a gray season: when they stopped speaking, they could hear nothing but the hum of motors and, from the valley, the distant whine of a training plane gently poised above the mist of the Meuse. The day was clear, but already cold: sounds carried very far.

"The Germans are clever, *mon yeutenant*." Olivon tossed his head with the stubborn, sullen look of a man who knows what he knows. "They have their tricks!"

They finished the bottle without much more talk. The tanks were now passing at longer invervals; the silence of the dim winter twilight fell on the forest again. As they stood up to return to the blockhouse, a motor behind them coughed and came to a stop: a light machine-gun tank pulled over to the side of the road, almost beside them, its artillery-gray outlines massive in the failing light. The driver and the officer in command jumped out, and, after poking around in the motor and gauging the gas supply, headed toward Grange, who had stopped to watch them under cover of the trees.

"We're out of gas," the sublieutenant said. "Is there a telephone around here we can use? I don't think anyone else will be coming this way," he added, making a face as he glanced behind him down the empty road.

There was no telephone line to Les Falizes. Grange sent Gourcuff, just returned, by bicycle to Moriarmé. The repair truck would not be up before two o'clock. Grange invited the stranded crew in and brought out a new bottle. In this army thirty years behind the times, motorization revived a whole forgotten hierarchy. With their diving helmets, their big goggles, their grease-stained monkey-suits, the cavalrymen somehow impressed Grange; he felt like a peasant before these turn-of-the-century chauffeurs who had stopped their thundering chariots at his roadside cottage for a drink.

"Not a bad little bungalow you've got here," the lieutenant remarked, whistling admiringly when they had climbed up the staircase. "And what do you do down there—raise mushrooms?"

The cavalrymen stared around the room and looked out the windows walled in by branches with a somewhat baffled expression.

Grange explained. The mystery of the blockhouses was an open secret, but the apathy of this army asleep on its feet somehow shielded the fact of their existence nevertheless: he knew that behind the Meuse no one, or almost no one, had heard of them. When he was through, there was a moment of silence in the room.

"Not bad, not bad at all," the lieutenant said rather coldly, obviously looking for something to say. He drew near the window and began to talk about hunting: the week before, at Les Houches, a man in his company had shot a boar that was about to charge his tank.

"I only hope you won't have bigger game to shoot at," Grange remarked politely.

They exchanged a few commonplaces, emptying the bottle. Grange felt uncomfortable; the lieutenant remained standing, and his eyes slipped toward the windows: a sickroom visitor suddenly tormented by his desire to escape to the fresh air outside. It had grown quite dark now.

"Why don't you show me the block," the lieutenant

said suddenly, in a tone that seemed to ask for a moment of confidential conversation.

The steps were wet and slippery: the drizzle had begun at nightfall. The flashlights made the blockhouse look still less appealing than by day. A cavelike suppuration trickled down the walls in great shiny sheets: occasionally in the humid darkness their boots cracked open the shell of one of the wood-snails that had crawled in through the embrasures. From the forest rose a heavy, viscous odor that stuck in Grange's throat—the moldy smell of walled-up cellars and mushroom beds.

"Quite a den you've got down here!" the lieutenant said, grimacing. He shuddered in the stagnant chill of the place and sniffed the exhausted air. His hand slid along the cannon's slender barrel and lifted the canvas hood off the breech. "It's like a mausoleum, isn't it? I hope the joke isn't too close for comfort," he said, his smile a trifle embarrassed.

"You get used to it," Grange said dryly, shrugging his shoulders. He no longer felt in a very good humor and was beginning to regret having invited the cavalrymen. "In your tanks, when the oil starts getting hot . . ."

"Yes, of course, it all depends on what you're used to," the lieutenant interrupted, his tone conciliatory. He glanced with interest at the embrasure. All the irony in his face was concentrated in the nostrils and the upper lip, which trembled slightly but continuously, like a rabbit's nose: this constant, creaturely sniffing irritated Grange: it was as if the man had scented a suspicion on the heavy air, something less material than an odor. From time to time the lieutenant glanced sidelong at Grange with a friendly wink that the place made vaguely sinister.

"What's that?" he asked, pointing to the tunnel hatchway.

Grange raised it: his flashlight revealed the first steps descending into the darkness; a faint smell of roots and wet earth rose from the opening.

"And you expect to stop the panzers like this?" the lieutenant resumed, thrusting his hands into his pockets and puffing out his cheeks, as if he found the notion prodigiously funny.

"I don't see how the tanks would get through the woods," Grange said, raising a hostile eyebrow. "And this will do some damage, anyway." He indicated the cannon breech with the tip of his boot.

"You won't have only tanks."

The lieutenant's voice had become crisp and precise, curiously impartial.

"You can keep your stovepipe and all that goes with it. Along with the first armored units you'll have engineers and motorized sections right away—and tough ones. And those bastards won't come by the road, either· they'll go around. They'll come and knock very politely at your bank-vault door, but after a couple of hand grenades you can say good night."

He glanced up at the ceiling again and tapped the wall with his fingernail, whistling ominously.

"We'll have to put mines around the blockhouse. And besides, what can *I* do about it?" Grange asked, shrugging his shoulders.

"Are you a reservist?"

Grange nodded.

"There's only one thing for you to do, my friend. . . ." He rested his hand lightly on Grange's shoulder and stared into his eyes, no longer joking. "Some good advice in return for your good wine: if I were you I'd arrange to get a transfer. You know what I'd call this little place they've rented for you out here in the woods? Don't let it upset you, but I'd call it a real hellhole. You'll be caught in here like a rat in a trap."

There was a moment of silence.

"I'm only telling you what I think." He smiled a little, almost courteously. "After all, you're out in the open here. You can always pray the good Lord they won't come."

A horn blew noisily on the road and they climbed out of the block. The repair truck had arrived; the cavalrymen said good-bye.

"I'll burn some sulphur in the block," Grange thought, exasperated. Fortunately no one else had been there. He felt deceived rather than in danger, like a man who discovers he has just lent all his money to a swindler.

THE autumn lingered on the heights of Les Falizes much longer than Grange had expected; after days of rain that turned the underbrush to jelly and stuck rafts of rotten leaves to their shoes, suddenly a dry, clear east wind swept the sky and hardened the roads, crackling the pin-oak leaves that still hung from the branches; it was as if a brisk and biting St. Martin's summer, already hemstitched with frost, had ventured into the very heart of December.

When Grange came downstairs to smoke his first cigarette outside after the morning coffee, there was a pearl of white frost on each blade of grass, but the branches were already dripping heavily onto the roadside shoulders. Above the forest, which looked, because of its oaks, as if it were still in leaf, a cold glassy sky hardened under the freshening wind. Grange liked this frost that made the roads firm again and carried all the way up to the blockhouse the whine of the little sawmill at Les Falizes and the crack of trees falling beneath the ax: on the road, where his steel-soled boots struck sparks from the gravel, the day smelled of fresh wood and flint—for a few minutes, he unconsciously breathed the morning's penetrating air with that almost ecstatic gaiety of wartime wakenings, the result of a renewed victory over fatigue, the tonic cold of the outdoors, the liberty of roads passable again. All the signs of approaching winter delighted him; he loved this sheltered season of deep sleep and short days: this was time embezzled with a bad conscience, but dearer than any other, like the magical vacations fire or epidemic grants to schoolboys.

On his way to Les Falizes now, Grange left the road where the clearing began and took a dirt path that ran between the forest and the thorn hedges of the little gardens: nothing pleased him more, when he had the whole day free, than to waken Mona, arriving in her house with the scent of the dewy morning still upon him. When he started very early, a pool of fog still lingered on the meadows, out of which emerged only the houses themselves, the hedge tops, and the clumps of the round apple trees. A thread of smoke already rose from the chimneys; sometimes a woman, wading through the fog along some invisible path, was hanging out her wash between the gardens at this first daylight hour. Grange had always associated happiness with an image of garden paths, and the war made it only all the more vivid: this night-washed alley, choked with fresh growth and edible abundance, now led to Mona too; he approached the clearing as if it were one of the Islands of the Blessed.

Mona's door was never locked—not so her lover could enter her house without wakening her, but because she belonged to that race of nomads tortured by the sound of a key in a lock: wherever she was, she always pitched her tent in the open air. When Grange came in, the square of grayish light from the open door fell on the brass table and the contents of her pockets which she had emptied there before going to bed: a jumble of keys, mint pastilles covered with lint, an agate marble, a tiny flask of perfume, a gnawed pencil stub, and seven or eight one-franc pieces. The rest of the room was very dim. Grange did not open the shutters right away, but noiselessly sat down near the bed, which emerged from the shadow, huge and dim, lit from below by the coals in the fireplace and the vague reflections from the brass andirons. When Mona awakened (she could also pass instantly from light to shadow, or from speech to sleep, falling asleep in the middle of a sentence, like a very young child), her wild caresses, her blows and bites, made Grange feel as though he were under an April shower; he was dispossessed of himself for the day; but this moment when he watched her still sleeping was more serious: sitting beside her, he had the feeling he was protecting her. The room grew chilly despite the dying fire; through the ill-fitting shutters filtered a gray dawn; for a moment he felt drawn into the heart of an extinguished world, ravaged by opposing stars, entirely controlled by some dark design: he glanced around him as if to look for the mortal wound that made the morning so pale, draining this dim chamber to the point of death. "Don't let her die," he murmured superstitiously, and the word wakened a vague echo in the shuttered room: the world had made its appeal and lost: as if, during its sleep, a listening ear had turned away.

Mona was lying flat on her belly, the covers heaped around her, her arms stretched out at full length, hands thrust beneath the pillow and gripping the bed on both sides; leaning over her, Grange smiled unconsciously, always amazed that even in its sleep this little body should cling so greedily to what it had already recognized as its need and comfort. Often she fell asleep naked; pulling up the sheet to cover her shoulders, Grange realized that this sudden, annihilating, childlike sleep of hers that astonished him so had mingled the recollection of a sweet subjection with the last moment of her exhaustion: it was as if a certain haste had borne her toward him across the long winter night, and something stirred within him at the thought: he quickly undressed without making a sound, and lay down beside her. Sometimes he slipped one arm beneath her, and curving the other around the pit of her belly, held her for a moment sleeping in his arms, wrapped in her roll of blankets: for

moments at a time, feeling the warmth of his full hands
rise to his shoulders along his tingling arms, he watched
her, marveling and intimidated, as if she were some baby
kidnaped in its swaddling clothes. He pressed his mouth
against her shoulder: she wakened in a second, clutched
him with both hands, and suddenly offered her insistent
forehead to his lips: she was a rain of tireless kisses, a
storm of tender gaiety, prodigal caresses.

He leaped naked from the bed to open the shutters
on a morning that had cleared now, where the fog was
already rising off the garden, and a great sheet of sunshine fell upon the sheets; drained, their bodies did not
separate: for hours together, drenched in the yellow sun
that stretched a shadowy network of branches across
the ceiling she lived and grew against him like a
tree espaliered on a wall. A sly finger scratched at the
door, and without waiting for a reply Julia appeared
with the steaming breakfast tray. Grange hurriedly
pulled up the sheet but Mona remained naked, sitting
up in the tangled bed, and Julia, leaning over to set down
the tray, gave a little throaty giggle at the sight of those
delicate breasts and that young belly emerging from the
foam of sheets as from the sea. "Her mistress," he
thought distractedly, and the word suddenly dissolved
all his feelings into a wild confusion: the bold eyes and
the smile on this other young and knowing mouth gave
Mona's kisses a kind of frenzy, a certain disorder . . .
Nothing puzzled him more than his hunger for her, in
which there was never satiety, nor weariness, and which

her first appearance, disturbing, ironic, so meagerly sensual, had utterly belied: he was obsessed with the idea that she had captured him, thrown him on her bed with this wild haste which left him breathless still; he read in it the signs of a genius for passion.

"In love," he told her, "you use Napoleon's tactics: you join battle, and see what happens afterwards." With one finger he played with the little gold cross she wore around her neck; he remembered how she said her prayers before going to sleep, like a good convent girl, and made Julia read aloud passages from the *Golden Legend* which she herself knew by heart. The first time he slept with her, while they were resting in the darkness, she had begun telling him quite spontaneously, with a kind of childish grace, the story of Saint Benedict and his sister Scholastica, who rejoiced because a storm had kept her brother near her and allowed her to profit by his conversation and his lessons. Outside, the heavy rain of the Ardennes battered the forest for miles and miles. It was all so unexpected, yet so charming. The extraordinarily childish tone was that of schoolgirls huddling together in some shelter against the downpour, telling each other stories until the storm had passed.

"But how did you know?" he asked sometimes with entranced perplexity, pressing her tiny head with its blue eyes and blond hair against his shoulder.

"You're not stupid," she answered, making her wise matron's face. She leaned back on one elbow and stared at him closely, shrewdly, putting a finger on his lips. "You're not stupid—but you're a little simple."

Even when they ate their lunch, she wound her legs in his, nibbled at his hand that stirred the coffee or reached for the sugar. "You're like a parrot," he told her, laughing and plunging his hand into the long mane that flowed like water down her back—"always hanging on by its beak and one foot." Then the nibbling became a bite; he pressed her against him, his nails digging into her flesh with a touch of madness that roused the taste for blood within him—at the same time that he watched the yellow spot of sunlight already sinking down the wall to the level of the bed. "So little time," he reminded himself with a kind of stupefaction—"I've so little time." He leaped out of the bed and hurriedly dressed: it was time for the truck to be at Les Falizes. The war always plunged Mona into an incredulous, indulgent astonishment.

"What can you do about it, *chéri*, in that house that's *so* ugly?" she would sometimes ask him while he was dressing. She watched him, her brows furrowed over a difficult idea, lying across the bed with both elbows propped on its edge, her chin deep in her hands, and suddenly these words separated him from her, disengaged him from his moorings: he felt as if a giant hull were floating beneath him, a vessel nothing could stop on its aimless course, already washed beyond recovery by the rhythm of the sea's breathing.

Back at Les Falizes, the rest of Grange's day loomed empty and exposed before him; even when he had no rendezvous with Mona, he never quite lost sight of the possibility that she might be there from one moment to the next: either she hitched a ride in the truck down to Moriarmé, or she took a walk in the woods with Julia—suddenly he would hear the light footsteps rushing up the blockhouse stairs: it was as if the slack had gone out of his life. Even her absence was easy for him to bear: he advanced into each of his days as down those airy seaside avenues where at each corner one unconsciously glances up to see if the vista still leads to the sea.

As well as supplies and mail, the truck also brought the newspapers from Moriarmé: often on the afternoons when he was expecting Mona in the blockhouse, Grange would sit at the window where he could lean out and look down the path, eager to see her a long way off, and while he was waiting he would examine the bundle of papers on his lap. His reasons for this interest were uncertain, and the result of his reading was like a well-mannered tedium; it was as if the dog days were being yawned away, the summer's orchestra relieved by an unexpected yet discreet entrance of the brasses, combining a taste for Sporting Events with the last sighs of Advice to the Lovelorn: *a group commander drowned in Lorient harbor while making a tour of inspection.——— Until 38, a love story, after 38, a life of glory: the heroic and legendary life of Kosciusko.———Why not play a few bars of La Marseillaise after God Save the King, General Spears asks the House of Commons.* This sickroom gossip circled a void that became almost dizzying: all at once a mysteriously allusive sentence gaping at the end of a paragraph made him wonder if a page had been torn out.

Here and there the war sputtered and smoked like an imperfectly extinguished forest fire; a breath of wind suddenly leaped over hundreds of miles, spreading sparks into the remotest Karelian forests. What could the war possibly be doing in Finland? Somewhere in the distance, under another sky, the world was listlessly continuing on its way, perhaps, and the reports of its progress did not seem very different from what they usually were; it was surprising, in fact, that a war should be so inhabitable— its gesticulation remained wordless, as if observed through plate glass, as if an enormous bell jar had been lowered over the heart of Europe, over the world's heart; he felt himself trapped beneath this bell, the exhausted air tight against his temples and his ears ringing.

From time to time Grange looked up from these papers heavy with lacunae and stared into the forest: he remembered the yellowed papers of 1914 which as a child he loved poring over in the attic—all full of that brutal, swaggering parade to the starting line, set off in front of an audience stunned by the starter's gun: how could *this* war infect the world with such a sleeping sickness? From time to time a dry leaf let go its hold and slipped noiselessly to the path, trivial in the cold, clear air, but what was coming was not winter's sleep but something more like the world that had collapsed at the approach of the millennium, sick at heart and everywhere abandoning its plows and harrows, waiting for signs. Not, Grange decided, that they were expecting the horsemen of the Apocalypse this time; as a matter of fact, they anticipated nothing at all, unless, already vaguely apprehended, that final sensation of falling free that cuts through the stomach in bad dreams and which, if you had tried to determine it more clearly—but you didn't really want to—might have been called the *end of the reel:* best, now, was the drunken sleep on the brink; never before had France pulled the sheet over her head with this feverish hand, this taste of nausea in her mouth.

When he had finished reading the papers, Grange poured himself a little coffee out of the pot on the stove and lit a cigarette. He did not settle down to reading at once (he had brought in his gear, along with a few detective novels—already devoured, but he reread them —a pocket Shakespeare, Gide's *Journal* which had just been published, and an English edition of Swedenborg's *Memorabilia*), but tried for a moment to conceive of the coming war, that is, forced himself to construct a somewhat plausible image of events which would involve the indefinite continuation of his encampment in the forest. It was not so much the danger of a real war that preoccupied him as it was *movement:* the worst disaster would be to have to leave the blockhouse. But, on the whole, chances were reasonably in his favor. The invasion of Belgium was unlikely: once was enough. Perhaps the Germans would attack through Switzerland— or else directly invest the Maginot Line: that would take a long time: a rather academic artillery duel, something like the siege of Paris in 1870, when families in their Sunday best would make a tour of the ramparts to collect shell splinters after Mass. Or else the question would be settled by the aviators. Sometimes he imagined two armies of sentinels indefinitely continuing their guard duty on each side of a border grown into a jungle of briars: this was the idea that pleased him the most; the recollection of *The Cossacks* provided a kind of poetry: it would be a primitive life, long drinking bouts, the companionship of forest vagabonds, nights in ambush among the wild beasts passing so close you could reach out and touch them. A certain measure of normal existence, in the long run, would not become impossible; but it would be more dangerous, wider awake, and the sound of gunfire would not necessarily mean someone hunting game. He would live here, with Mona.

"Yes, who knows?" he told himself, squinting a little against this surge of blind joy he had never experienced before. It alarmed him—and he hurriedly rapped his fingers on the raw wood table: several weeks ago he had started becoming superstitious. Yet even this dream did not comfort him long: it was the body's pseudo-sleep when the rhythm of the night train rocks it back and forth in its seat.

From his post at the window, he caught sight of Mona at the turn of the path from Les Falizes, half a mile away —a tiny black speck that seemed to hesitate a moment in the distance, then changed its course and glided toward the blockhouse: he was certain it was Mona—there were people on the road only at certain hours and Grange knew them all. Sometimes another black speck, which was Julia, kept her company: from as far off as possible he tried to make out which was Mona, and even before any detail was discernible he recognized her by her freer, lighter step, her way of slipping along the path like a boat surrendering itself to the current's pressure. On each side of the white road stretched the empty woods that glowed now as far as the eye could reach with a tawny cast beneath the huge sky: around him, he felt the world disturbed and dark, in the image of this troubled forest, but before him lay that road: it seemed as if she were coming to him by a road opened in the sea.

Nights in the forest were not always so calm now. Orders had come from Moriarmé to check all clandestine crossings of the frontier between the blockhouses; a series of night patrols was instituted, and the blockhouse at Les Falizes was often alerted for this duty by the morning supply truck. All the men had volunteered for these nocturnal excursions; they were pleased that the service had become more active; too dead a calm was ominous, but this night watch officially established them in an inoffensive war: it was reassuring. Grange preferred taking Hervouët along because of his taciturn disposition and his almost feline agility. They slipped out of the blockhouse on a night so calm that as they walked down the road they heard a distant church in the valley strike eleven, the notes rich and heavy despite the distance, then, distinctly nearer, the slightly cracked chimes of a Belgian steeple. They followed the road for half a mile; beyond a turn, the trees suddenly clustered around and above the road, plunging it into a deep hollow where an odor of moss and stagnant water floated on the darkness. The outer rim of this shadowy thicket marked the frontier; they stopped here to light a cigarette and smoke in silence for a moment at the brim of sleeping Belgium, like strollers whose path ends at the cliff's edge. The grove was pitch dark—a few steps from Grange everything vanished into the black underbrush which cast still thicker shadows; he noticed only the glowing tip of a cigarette next to him, and heard the click of the cartridge Hervouët was slipping into his pistol. Then the silence of the place became almost magical. A strange feeling ran through him each time he lit a cigarette in this forgotten wilderness; it was as if he were slipping his moorings; he entered a world redeemed, rid of men, pressed against its starry sky with that same dizzying swell of the empty sea. "I'm alone in the world," he told himself rapturously.

Sometimes the two men stood there for a long time, saying nothing. Beyond the frontier the forest emitted a few vague noises—which they unconsciously strained to hear—like the uninterpretable flotsam the sea washes up on a beach and which the eye mechanically fixes on: this dimly wakened border where the patrolled forests of the war harbored a fabulous, enchanted silence that was somehow alive and alert fascinated Grange, intrigued him. Hervouët threw away his cigarette and drank a few mouthfuls from his canteen: they left the road and turned down a service path that closely paralleled the frontier for some distance. From this moment on, they ceased speaking entirely, advancing, hunched over, along what seemed an improvised though already ancient trail carpeted with rotten leaves that muffled their footsteps. When Grange pointed his flashlight ahead of him and turned it on, the cone of light suddenly revealed the low branches that wove themselves into a vault of slender twigs above the path: they trudged on, as lost here as a flea in the roots of a fur pelt; when Grange switched off the flashlight a long, faintly phosphorescent streak appeared in the treetops overhead, where the darkness had been thickest. As they advanced, the night changed: the midnight sluggishness gradually mounted above the trees, and a lighter atmosphere infused the underbrush with a vapory blue incense; the moon was rising and made the land passable as far as the eye could reach, as gently as the sun, appearing among clouds, dries the rainy roads. Behind him, Grange heard only Hervouët's footsteps, occasionally making the dry branches snap, and the regular clicking of his bayonet sheath which resumed each time he released it to drink out of his canteen. Shining his flashlight left toward the heart of the forest, Grange could see the gleaming wires beaded with dew and the stakes of the low network that ran along the frontier at ground level—several pairs of eyes shone for a second, caught in the beam of light, and they heard the rabbits' tiny thunder rush across the leaves. To the right, his eyes followed a long reach of the forest descending in ravines toward the Meuse; a shy moon sailed high above the black woods; burdened by the cold, circles of smoke from the charcoal burners' fires floated in large gray puddles that gently revolved over the trees, their edges rising with the slow, circular motion of jellyfish. Grange watched, his forehead lined with concentration and a mysterious expectancy. There was a powerful charm in standing here, so long after midnight had sounded from the earth's churches, deep in this placeless gelatin masked by pools of fog and steeped in the vague sweat of dreams, at the hour when the mist floated out of the forest like spirits. Grange gestured to Hervouët and both men held their breath for a moment, listening to the great respiration of the woods around them that made a kind of low and intermittent music, the long, deep murmur of an undertow that came from the groves of firs near Les Fraitures; over this tidal undulation they could hear the crackle of branches along some nocturnal creature's course, the trickling of a spring, or sometimes a dog's high-pitched howl roused by the moon, such sounds rising at one moment or another out of the smoking vat of the forest. As far as the eye could reach a fine blue vapor floated over the forest—not the dense fumes of sleep but rather a lucid, quickening exhalation that disengaged the mind, making all the paths of insomnia dance before it. The dry and sonorous night slept with its eyes wide open; the secretly wakened earth was full of portents once again, as in the age when shields were hung in the branches of oaks.

Behind the pine grove of Les Fraitures, they followed a

ravine back to the highway and sat down on the roadside grass, smoking in silence until they heard footsteps on the asphalt beyond the bend: the patrol from the block-house of Les Buttés. Grange's mind felt marvelously clear; a marrow-piercing cold rose from the earth in the small hours of the morning; squatting on the grass in his overcoat, he concentrated entirely on the aroma of the hot coffee Lieutenant Lavaud, a man of prudence, would pour him out of his thermos. There was a certain fitness that the war should announce itself this way, in a clash of raw sensations. Sometimes, when the patrol was late, Grange dozed off a little despite his hunger, and almost at once began dreaming where he crouched on the frozen grass. It was almost always a dream of roads. He dreamed of tanks rolling toward the blockhouse down the long forest road in front of the embrasure. He dreamed of what was to happen.

When the night was clear and the roads dry, Grange left Hervouët where the service path turned off under the great oaks and sent him back to the blockhouse; he kept on straight ahead, taking a short cut through a grove of young pines to Les Falizes: from this side, he reached the clearing through cherry orchards and alfalfa beds where the stone rollers lying in the grass raised their shafts to the moon. Grange jumped over the stiles and crossed the gardens to the door of Mona's little house; before opening it, he wrapped his handkerchief around the old wrought-iron lock in order not to waken her; even from the threshold, crouching deep in the shadows where the moonlight struck steely reflections from the furniture, he could hear the long, light breathing that rose to meet his own fatigue. The pot-bellied wardrobes smelled of lavender; through the open door he could see the first few pear trees that lined the alley, their branches stiff as corals in the moonlight. He sat down beside Mona's sleeping body and covered her shoulders with the red patchwork quilt which had slipped to the floor: like a sleeping kitten sharpening its claws on the rags in its basket, Mona could sleep comfortably only after creating terrible carnage among the bedclothes.

He did not awaken her as she lay hidden by the darkness, submerged in a mysterious, remote comfort; he did not even look at her. Pressed against her hip, he heard only her long breathing, and through the open door the great tidal murmur of the pines at Les Fraitures fading away in the distance. It seemed as if his life were no longer divided, partitioned, as if everything were of a piece because of one door left ajar that blurred the hours of sleep with those of daylight and cast him upon Mona from the heart of the war's watchful night. He closed his eyes a second and listened in the darkness to their mingled breathing, rising and falling against the long, low rustle of the forest: it was like the sound of ripples deep in a cave, the backwash against the clamor of the breakers; the same enormous impulse of the tide that swept the earth raised them in its swell, bearing sleep and waking onward together. Before leaving, Grange brushed his finger tips across the moist hollow of Mona's hand which lay open in her sleep, palm upward in the darkness, seeking some blind acquiescence, an acknowledgment that left him appeased.

Returning to the blockhouse along the road, he saw the spotlights above the Meuse valley still bright against the first gleams of dawn: the work continued by day as well as by night. The casements were further along now. An advance unit of the Engineers had been encamped near Les Buttés, and Moriarmé sent word that during the month following road blocks would be installed and mine fields laid around the blockhouse, as provided for.

IT WAS toward the end of December that the first snow fell on the Ardennes. When Grange awakened, a white and sourceless light oozed up from the earth, blurring the shadow of the windowframes against the ceiling; but his first impression was less that of unaccustomed brightness than of an abnormal suspension of time itself: at first he thought his alarm clock had stopped; the room, the whole house, seemed to be soaring down a long landslide of silence—a delicious, downy, cloistral silence that would never be broken. He got up, saw the forest white as far as the eye could reach, and lay down again in his noiseless room with a joy so great it made him blink. The silence around him was even subtler in this luxuriant light. Time came to a stop: for the inhabitants of the Roof, this magical snow that closed the roads opened the long vacation.

Communications with Moriarmé were soon severed almost entirely. The wheezing supply truck, despite the chains on its tires, after floundering once or twice in the drifts, rarely risked crossing the icy slopes of l'Eclaterie. Every two days, Gourcuff, ballasted with a canteen of brandy and armed with knapsacks, trudged down to the battalion headquarters: he came back very late, very red, very drunk, his knapsacks bulging with mail, cans of food, and bags of biscuits. The blockhouse crew, field glasses trained on his premonitory zigzags in the failing light, encouraged him up the last few hundred yards with an anticipatory concert of mugs and canteens clashed together.

"Come on, Gourcuff, give it the gas!" Hervouët shouted, while the black shape staggered through the snow, magically increasing its speed. In the Meuse army, almost all the slang was motorized.

They hoisted him up the iron staircase into the common room, where Olivon pushed him into a chair with its back to the glowing stove and "defrosted" him with a mugful of the hot grog that now replaced the coffee in the pot. A cloud of vapor rose from Gourcuff's clothes while a pool spread under his chair—then he sneezed with a kind of majesty, and a rainbow of curious distillations volatilized in the room.

"Worse than a locomotive, with all that steam," Olivon declared with an admiring whistle, clapping him on the back. "But you've got to admit he burns up a lot. . . ."

In his office in Moriarmé, the snow made Varin increasingly gloomy. The first bad weather clogged the joints of this wheezing army, stalled the rattletrap engines that were scarcely serviceable for summer maneuvers. Over six inches of snow and construction, convoys, maneuvers, transport, communications, target practice—all the daily grindings and gnashings of machinery stopped as though bewitched: the roof garrison became a horde stupefied by hibernation, little groups burrowing into the warm holes of their stoves and igloos. The orders slept, unopened, on the captain's desk. After having asked without much conviction for "ski troops" and "high-altitude materiel," Varin threw up his arms and began talking with glum distaste of "living off the country." The captain's tone comprised a whole Retreat from Moscow. The men, divining their present freedom, were ecstatic. They had not enjoyed the image of what lay before them, that last, all too likely battle they advanced toward with all the slow enthusiasm of a Percheron between its shafts: as soon as they felt the reins slacken, they too thrust their noses into the roadside grass, looking for the ostrich's sand-buried dreams. And beneath this soft snow which smoothed the earth and masked all roads, they nursed a vague illusion of making themselves invisible, of giving fate the slip.

The snow conferred on this low and shaggy Ardennes

forest a charm which even the lofty mountain treetops
or the Vosges firs do not possess for all their ice candles.
Across these short, stiff twigs, the white ropes of snow
hung unbroken for weeks at a time, welded to the bark
by tiny wads of ice that were the melted drops seized in
their fall by the long night's cold: for whole days at a
time, in air decanted by the freeze, the Roof covered itself with dust-sheets, pale bundles, gossamers, and the
long white lace of frosty mornings. A violent blue sky
glistened over this holiday landscape. The air was piercing but almost warm; at noon, from each patch of sun
that made the snow sparkle, you could hear the slow
gurgle rising from the thaw's entrails, but as soon as the
short twilight reddened the horizon toward the Meuse,
the cold again brought a magical suspense to the Roof:
the sealed forest became a snare of silence, a winter
garden whose barricades yielded only to the comings and
goings of ghosts. For the snow clung to the faintest
gleams of light, and even by night the uplands of the
Meuse seemed alive; often, now, behind the aureoles of
the concrete mixers, the anti-aircraft searchlights swept
the forest sky beyond the frontier with their quadruple
bars of light, and a phosphorescence glowed and faded
across the snow between the coal-black trunks, like the
sudden gentle flames that devour a wad of cotton. These
northern lights, this glory of glacial illumination which
explored the empty night and seemed to sharpen the cold,
made place and season alike look unfamiliar. Sometimes
the beams crossing his uncurtained window wakened

Grange during the night, like the lighthouse that had brushed across his panes on that Breton island where he had slept so badly; he got up, leaned on the sill, and for a moment watched the strange columns of light slowly, warily wheeling in the winter sky; then an image from his childhood reading occurred to him; he remembered H. G. Wells' sick Martian giants screaming their incomprehensible woes across the stupefied landscape.

But as soon as these signs had faded with the darkness from the sky, the Roof returned to its rude activities. Before the sun was up, Grange heard outside his window the crackling of a great fire of brambles Olivon lit beneath the washtub to melt the morning ice; the men soon gathered around its sudden heat; sometimes a woodcutter stopped on his way to work from Les Falizes to warm his hands before the blaze. Grange liked hearing this murmur beneath his window, when *his house* began to hum for the whole day: ever since the snow, his relations with Moriarmé had become more and more those of a vassal who has chosen to raise his drawbridge and keep his distance. The blockhouse no longer lived on the valley: the cans of food and the biscuits Gourcuff brought up from Moriarmé had accumulated in the concrete block below, constituting a kind of private siege stock whose arrangement Grange and Olivon went down to inspect from time to time.

"We're pretty well fixed," Olivon said, nodding at the heaped larder: and his tone was that of a steward checking the storeroom of a ship caught in an ice floe. There was a suggestion in it of the magical wish that they might be forgotten here for a long time—forever.

Grange had arrived at Moriarmé with quite a lot of money in his wallet which the blockhouse life and his accumulated pay had increased month by month: Les Falizes replaced the Commissariat, though it had neither bakery nor grocery; the farms, provisioned for the long plateau winter and still baking their own bread, furnished all the food they needed, and there was no lack of wine either. The money slipped happily between his fingers. "The hell with saving," he decided with a shrug of the shoulders. "We'll see later on. In the spring . . ." and against the back of his neck—half-apprehension, half-excitement—he felt a faint prickle, like the roller-coaster rider who sees, not far ahead, the curve of the big plunge approaching.

Never before had he felt his life so open and warm as it seemed this winter on the Roof, free of ties, isolated from past and future alike by crevasses as deep as those that separate the pages of a book. However lightly he might have felt himself committed to his life, the war had severed the few links he recognized: in 1914 for the last time, perhaps, men had left home with the idea of return- ing *for the harvest*; in 1939 they had exchanged their country dances for the movies, but it was without looking back that they left, knowing in their heart of hearts they would see only a land the fire had passed over. No sooner had they abandoned it than the life which still enveloped them in all its warmth seemed tainted with a swift, an irremediable aging—withered in the stalk, already too white for harvest. Before him stretched this curtain—lowered still but stirred now by mysterious currents, pierced by sudden beams, and he sensed the footlights were about to come up. Until then, between the old life and whatever was behind the curtain, the time to come was comforting. The earth had grown buoyant again; once winter had come, the sick and the old, in the wake of the evacuated rest home, had one after the other decamped from the forest villages, disappearing behind the lines in the smoke of the wheezing little Meuse trains: the Roof was rejuvenated, like a city after a siege during which it has abandoned its *useless mouths*. However little martial spirit he thought he possessed, Grange nevertheless sensed—obscurely, powerfully—the war's bitter, rousing spring in this brutal sweep of the broom that cleared the earth of its offal: the air that bathed these outposts now was livelier than a forecastle breeze.

The snow, cutting off the blockhouse from the Meuse, brought it closer to Les Falizes. Now that the ancients of the tribe had left the plateau, which the war had already emptied of its able-bodied men, only the freest, shrillest feminine laughter sounded on the snowy slopes from morning to night, and matters were arranged simply. The tastes of the blockhouse occupants tended on the whole toward consistency and stability, and the Christmas landscape, the long nights, the uncertainty of the time to come, as well as a certain peasant seriousness of character apparent in both Olivon and Hervouët, gave the men a kind of nostalgia for *a woman by the fireside*.

Olivon could generally be found at Les Platanes, where Gourcuff occasionally helped him with the bottling, actually quite infrequent now that Grange had become almost the only customer. When he came in for his afternoon coffee, he often surprised Olivon sitting under the *Byrrh* calendar and wearing a jute apron (the apron of the deceased, Grange reflected: the café-owner was a rather heavy-set though still agreeably cheerful widow), explaining the morning paper to Madame Tranet—an occupation of considerable significance, since it was Olivon who decoded the second page of the *Communiqués de la Prefecture*, which set subtle traps for winesellers in these difficult times.

Hervouët replaced *chasseur alpin* in the house of a farm woman so pale and so thin, so overwhelmed by her large family and hard times, that the public opinion of Les Falizes had not taken the family's new provider in bad part, and Hervouët's appearance at Les Mazures was regarded as the mission of a heaven-sent paladin who consecrated himself to the protection of widows and orphans.

Grange, whom this exemplary interim sometimes perplexed a little, grew calm again at the thought that his orders—beyond the service itself—prescribed after all the most generous use of the garrison for agricultural work. Seen early in the morning chopping the day's wood, breaking the ice in the well and shoveling the snow away from the door long before the rest of the

household was up, his functions—rather serious and
dignified ones on the whole, marked with the character of
necessity—so far outstripped more playful suggestions
that order was somehow re-established and readjusted of
its own accord: it might be said that Hervouët was justified by his works. In thinking about the avatars of his
little world, Grange, vaguely touched, was not far from
feeling that he was on the whole *well settled*. It was only
Gourcuff who gave him any concern now, crippled by
Hervouët's secession and flaunting a strangely arrogant
alcoholic chastity around the blockhouse. During his
hours of liberty, he would disappear down some snow-
clogged path, always alone, always sweating, and always
very red, furiously punching his helmet down on his
head and muttering Breton oaths into the raised collar of
his overcoat.

"He's hunting," Olivon said, winking mysteriously
and assuming the complacent tone of a retired family
man.

What astonished Grange was that these haphazard
couples created an image that was quite the contrary of
licentiousness; surprisingly, the domestic routine of the
blockhouse, the sort of liberal discipline which had been
established there, did not suffer from it in any way. The
blockhouse, in fact, filled a place left empty; it restored,
in the village—surrendered entirely to the vagaries of
women—a male order that involved an unaccustomed
severity of behavior, for if it included the bed, it did not
extend to the evening paper and slippers. As soon as the

abrupt winter twilight set in, the members of the little
crew buckled their belts, shook the dust out of their
overcoats onto their women's doorsteps, and returned for
the night, their own masters, to the *men's house*, as in the
Carib villages, where everything belonged to another
order: language, mood, topics, jokes. It was a fragile
world, hanging over the void on all sides, but somehow
its machinery managed to function nevertheless. Occasionally Grange was reminded of a stopped clock set
running again by an earthquake, though sounding only
on the quarter-hour: he had always delighted in such
mechanisms, costing a penny or lasting a day, delicate
and absurd, where chance momentarily made necessity
flourish once again. When he was entirely honest with
himself, he reflected that these almost creaturely romances of their billetings, winter-hatched and blooming
quite apart in the warm comfort of the houses, reassured him: they made his feeling for Mona turn toward
a peaceable order, gave it a certain solidity, even a kind
of hope.

He got up early now to finish off the few tasks the
curbed life of the blockhouse still required, well before a
light the color of dirty water, grayer than the ground,
began to filter through the woods ahead of the sun: an
image of Mona's house taking its dust-bath in the still-
dark morning sharpened his appetite. He left Olivon in
charge and started down the road, almost the whole day
ahead of him. The white earth crackled again beneath its
frozen crust; night withdrew from the forest without a

breath of wind, as if swallowed by the snow; before he reached the path to Les Falizes, a great red sun rose in front of him down the road's long vista. This moment always seemed fresh and marvelous to Grange: the air was even more alive and tingling than his own coursing blood; it was as if the day had never dawned so young before. He rapped his iron-tipped stick against Mona's door, feeling as good-humored as if he had swallowed a flask of brandy before setting off on his expedition. With her short sheepskin-lined jacket, her heavy rubber boots, her yellow hair that looked as tangled as if she had been sleeping on the ground and still seemed to have bits of straw in its meshes, as fresh as the scrubbed red tiles of the house itself, Mona gave off a rough, wholesome smell, reminding him of the grass broom and the currycomb, or washing in the horse trough. Outside, nothing could be heard but the thaw's great drops drumming from the eaves and the cocks crowing in the already sun-drenched morning. Mona was always on time; each morning she emerged from the darkness as fresh and pale as a beach when the tide recedes.

"How old are you?" he would ask her sometimes, stroking her eyebrows with his finger, staggered by her beauty, blinking as if into too bright a light while she laughed her throaty laugh and lightly ruffled his hair—but he realized that his question had no meaning, that youth, here, had nothing to do with age; she belonged to a fabulous species, like unicorns. "I found her in the woods," he mused, and a certain wonder touched his heart; there was a sign upon her: the sea had floated her to him on a stone slab; he felt how precariously she was granted; the waves that had brought her would take her back again.

They turned into a path behind the naked gardens and frozen cabbage patches leading to Les Fraitures. As soon as they had left Les Falizes behind, the landscape revealed itself; the path followed the lip of the great slope of woods that dipped toward Belgium. At the end of the forest, black against the snow, that reached the horizon without one house, without one column of smoke, they could see a town clinging to a peak over a gorge, its white houses sparkling in the sun above the mauve fog. The light reflected from the snow gave it the phosphorescence of a forbidden city and a promised land. The sun mounted higher, sending a rain of drops from every branch, but for a long time, as they walked toward Les Fraitures, the town on the brink of its gorge sparkled gloriously between the white and the blue. Mona was sure it was Spa: ever since she had read the name, which enchanted her, on the waiting-room posters, she could not believe there were any other towns in the Belgian Ardennes.

"Why don't you take me?" she asked, shaking his arm with that insistence of desire that seemed to turn the world new again each time. And nodding with a knowing housewifely precocity, added: "Julia could come with us. In Belgium, you know, it's not very expensive."

Beyond the gorge of Les Fraitures, they shoveled the

night's accumulated snow away from the door of an abandoned charcoal burner's cottage and pulled out the *luge*, a kind of heavy sleigh or *schlitte* used to haul logs through the forest. The Bihoreau boy, whose proficiencies ranged from electrical repairs to pottery mending, had fitted it with cane-bottomed seats; though it was clumsy and quite heavy, they pulled the sleigh through the pines as far as the Fraitures Light, a pylon made of unbarked tree trunks standing in a clearing at the top of the hill. The ten o'clock sun spangled the frozen snow, and Grange and Mona laughed at the two great clouds of breath they puffed before them as they walked. When they reached the pylon, they ate some of the food Julia had prepared and which Mona was carrying in a knapsack. Mona always tied the sleigh to the pylon, like a horse: it was one of her eccentricities—like unlocked doors and sudden signs of the cross made with her thumb —which Grange dared not question; in his moments of enthusiasm, he was not far from believing she possessed the secret of certain half-magical practices of primitive life. Admitted to her intimacy, he was far from knowing everything about her: there were still moments when she frightened him.

On the steep flank of the hill, a clearing in the woods opened ahead of them, wide and rectangular. The sleigh started gradually over the fresh snow, then, with the acceleration of an avalanche, plunged straight down, scraping its bottom on the black roots of the roughly cleared hillside: the sun, the powdery snow, the treacherous snags, the nearby cliff of black pines, everything in Grange's vision was swallowed up in the wake of a violent wind that tore at his ears and seemed to purge the earth of all weight; he felt Mona's breasts—she was lying upon him—lightly crushed against his back, then released at every jolt of the sleigh; she clung to his shoulders, light and warm as the troll children you carry across the ford and whose weight suddenly buckles your legs. Sometimes the sport became stranger still: he felt Mona's cold teeth close on the nape of his neck and her hands slide along his arms to his wrists, which were steering. The sleigh tumbled them gently into a snowbank which the stream at the bottom of the ravine was undermining; rolled into the drift, weak with laughter, they struggled, arms and knees pressed together, and suddenly he felt Mona's teeth against his nape a second time: a sudden weakness ran through his body, like that of a cat lifted off the ground by the skin of its neck—the snow, which slipped into the hollow of his shoulders and down his arms, became a soft burning. When they shook themselves and sat down a moment on the sleigh to catch their breath, he glanced at her, her waist so slender in her close-fitting blouse, with a shadow of anxiety; he thought of those wasps which instinctively know where to sting in order to paralyze their prey. As soon as they had stopped talking, their eyes closed, they heard only the faint gurgle of the thaw, and sometimes, far away, a lonely cock shrilled to the noonday sun: his head against Mona's shoulder, Grange felt the world come to him crammed with a tender profusion.

By the time they returned to the hut and ate what remained of their food sitting side by side on the sleigh, the afternoon was already getting on; the forest horizon darkened, surmounted by a band of mauve. The cold increased, and a touch of mournfulness appeared in the slanting light. Mona shivered beneath her short furred jacket: she clouded over as suddenly as any mountain sky, immediately exposed to the warnings of the hour and the season.

"I don't like this time of day," she said, shaking her head when he questioned her. And when he asked what she was thinking about: "I don't know. About death. . . ." Then she would lean her head on his shoulder, and momentarily give herself up to strange, hurried sobs, as sudden as an April shower. He felt the cold seize him roughly now. He did not like the words that rose to this child-sibyl's mouth, suddenly so full of darkness.

When they reached Les Falizes, a cold blue shadow lay across the walls; threads of ice, already frozen again at the gutter rims, silenced the alleys between houses. Even before the sun had set, the snow turned gray. The earth around them suddenly seemed so dim, so frozen, that Mona's forebodings spread to Grange: he felt the day collapse at the bottom of a black pit, and a gray, cold liquid rose within him, its taste stale in his mouth. As soon as Julia had served tea, they undressed with anxious haste; in the great darkened room, weighted with the evening's sadness, they embraced without speaking a word. Sometimes Grange half sat up between the cold sheets, and letting go Mona's fingers, stared, his eyes wide open, toward the thick clumps of shadow that invaded the room. "What's the matter with me?" he wondered, his heart heavy. "Who knows? It's *twilight nerves*," but he was surprised never to have had them before. When he came back to the blockhouse at nightfall, his solitude depressed him; often he would call for Hervouët at Les Mazures before returning. They set out along the wet snow path that sponged up all sounds. As soon as they turned into the road, the glow from the other side of the Meuse, which outshone the twilight now, released across the sheets of snow a sickly phosphorescence, a kind of false dawn. It seemed to Grange that the earth itself was yellowing with disease, that time was working there, underneath, with a slow fever: they walked upon it as on a corpse that was beginning to smell.

OFTEN, back in his room, he found on his desk the mail which Gourcuff or the occasional supply truck had brought up from battalion headquarters, and this prospect darkened his returns: he did not enjoy the news any more: he was like those solitary creatures who have left a mother or an older sister somewhere and who slyly avoid the postman every day. If Grange came in late, the silence from the crew room, a silence not that of sleep, told him even before going into his room that the newspapers had come up from Moriarmé, and scarcely more than a minute passed before Olivon knocked at his door, supposedly to *report* (according to the evidence of an unaccustomed and hypocritical heel-clicking that Grange found cheering) but in fact only to return to the crew room with the pacifying news that "the lieutenant seemed in a good mood."

But there seemed, in fact, to be no cause for alarm. Apparently nothing in the official communications indicated that a change in the Roof sector was imminent. With a little optimism, one could occasionally pick up hints that were frankly reassuring; for example that communication from the engineers—already promising a long spring lull—which ordered the anti-tank mines to be removed after the thaw for checking and stocking. Yet something filtered through this grayish logorrhea—more abundant each week—which spoiled his calm a little: as if a mind given over to sleep were still obsessed with its heavy thoughts, occasionally rousing the nerve ends with tiny twinges. Now that the winter was advancing, it was the *cavalry* maneuvers that seemed to worry him, for everyone knew (the cavalrymen themselves made no secret of it) that in case of a German attack the cavalry was to deploy its units far ahead of the lines in Belgium. But when he tried to decipher the extremely fragmentary orders that reached Les Falizes, Grange was astonished by the perspective that appeared: obviously the cavalry's advance ahead of the lines mattered less than its manner of retreat behind them. Week after week a hail of detailed orders on this point alerted the Meuse unit-commanders in their snowbound posts, specifying retreat itineraries, the order of flow of the columns, and the units authorized to set off the detonations. The transfer of the blockhouses to the command of the retreating cavalry crossing the frontier was spelled out with special precision. Grange received diagrams indicating in red pencil on the master plans the fire zone of the advanced artillery provided to cover the cavalry retreat behind the Meuse. "The Meuse?" Grange reflected—and it was as if a long, sly brush had touched the blockhouse in the obscurity of its forest, making it gleam with a dangerous phosphorescence—"the Meuse?" This had something to do with them.

He leaned on the table and drummed his finger tips against the black window, quite bewildered. After this disagreeable shock, a reflex system of compensatory speculations began to function. He could hardly conceive that the war would knock at the blockhouse door one of these days: in this ponderous military machinery, every cog frozen solid in the earth, action of any kind assumed for the imagination the abnormal aspect, prepared for in advance, of a moving day. "Besides, who even wants to talk about it?" Grange asked himself, shrugging his shoulders. "No one takes such things seriously. Why, even in conversations at Moriarmé . . ." and here he stopped short, remembering Varin ("But Varin! . . ." he thought). Unfortunately, shrugging his shoulders did not get rid of everything; something remained: an anxiety he could neither localize nor reduce, the same disturbance, he decided, that kept his men from falling asleep on the nights there were "papers" on his desk. When he had finished reading *Le Petit Ardennais* and the newspapers from Paris, Grange sometimes wondered what accounted for his stubborn impression that "the newspapers were so bad." Nothing was happening. The war in Finland was obviously drawing to a close. In the east, which had caused a lot of talk for a while, everything seemed calm: the Caucasus oil wells still refused to go up in flames. These alarms had been so many backfires which, after having briefly reddened the horizon, burnt down and went out one after the other. And now, on the northeast front, the silence was beginning to grow a little ominous—broken only by discreet coughs and sounds of chairs being moved, by which guests indicate that time is weighing heavily, almost indecorously, between the hors-d'œuvre and the appearance of a more substantial course. For this silence, now distinctly irritating, was a hunger, and yawning made him think not so much of boredom as of the fearful gape of jaws which meant something quite different. The winter was growing old—he felt its peace cracking like the floating island in Jules Verne which, day by day, the thaw diminished.

When he had wrestled a while with these joyless thoughts the night provoked—his Larvae, as he called them—he would glance at the map of Belgium tacked over his bed—compliments of the *Petit Ardennais*—printed in three colors and surrounded by a fringe of French, German, and Belgian flags with perforated outlines, to be used at the appropriate moment for marking the fronts: it was as if, Grange thought, frowning with surprise each time it occurred to him—as if a circle of flies were waiting around a cheese for the glass bell to be raised. Soberly he measured a few distances, using his nail file and the scale at the corner of the map. On the whole, the Belgian buffer wasn't very thick. From the German frontier to the Meuse, it was probably little less than a hundred kilometers: three hours on the road, driving slowly. Luckily, these were Ardennes kilometers, allergic to armies, as anyone could see: in 1914 Joffre had come to grief over them and the lesson had not been wasted. Grange observed with satisfaction the enormous green stain which thrust its tentacles from Liége to beyond the Meuse; as far as forests went, it was about as serious an obstacle as you could find; he noticed, moreover, that nowhere was it more compact than opposite Les Falizes. "Not a single clearing!" he sighed with a secret *satisfecit* that drew up the corners of his mouth. Besides, there were references. "An enormous forest of small trees," Michelet had written: an army did not go counter to such great, placid evidences. Worse than a forest, really: a jungle. And there was the Belgian army to reckon with besides: seventeen divisions. They must have prepared formidable defenses. "The forest roads," he dreamed on, scowling. "With a few barbwire emplacements! . . ."; the trouble was, he suddenly realized, that the trees *were* so small—but you couldn't have all the luck on your side. He thought for another moment, under his blankets, about the Belgian army, about the forest, about the tank traps and barbwire emplacements, about the lessons of history. If someone had reminded him of the curious for-

getfulness that put the Army of the Meuse between pa-
rentheses, he would have been rather shocked. He never
thought of it, that was all, strange as it seemed—and
probably he would not have enjoyed exploring his
motives. Half dozing already, he listened calmly to the
forest growing.

TOWARD the middle of January, after snowfalls which rendered the roads entirely impracticable, the weather cleared and a German reconnaissance plane appeared at lunchtime over the Meuse valley. It was only a tiny silver speck, occasionally glistening in the sun as the distance slowed its progress to a crawl across the sky; a languid trail of globular puffs followed behind at some distance, blooming in its wake with a cottony "plop." The spectacle seemed not in the least warlike to Grange, but rather ornamental, graceful: the bursts were as regularly spaced one behind the other as if the clear morning sky had been neatly planted by some celestial dibble. The airplane returned almost every day for a week. Grange decided the snow showed up the earthworks under construction along the Meuse more clearly: the Germans were profiting by this condition to take photographs. As the coffee was served in the blockhouse, the odd, irregular buzzing made every head turn toward the windows.

"What a trick!" Gourcuff murmured, winking broadly toward the plane. He sheltered his eyes comically with his helmet, as if against the sun, actually protecting himself against the shell splinters that sometimes tinkled off the roof slates. But the anti-aircraft crews never hit the plane: they were using the same .75 caliber that had taken pot shots at the *Taubes* during the last war.

"Old equipment!" Olivon sighed, impartial and bored, lifting his cup again. Again they heard, for a moment, the heavy oily "plop" exploding gently in the calm blue air with the prudent rhythm of an official salute.

Varin must be going out of his mind, Grange thought. After the reconnaissance, he must be expecting the attack any day now. Grange imagined the captain prowling up and down his office, his hands behind his back, with that insolent way he had of suddenly planting himself in front of his interlocutor, nostrils flaring, his mouth a little twisted: "You still don't see?" On certain days, the world back of the blockhouse melted into the fog altogether, but never Varin: he remained terribly distinct, perhaps because of the shiny nickel-plated telephone on his desk and the nervous hand, quicker than a cat's paw, that picked up the receiver, cutting off the first ring;

Grange could imagine the *big push* only vaguely save for one image that was extraordinarily precise: Varin's thin hand on the telephone and the avid, nervous twitch of his lips which were all that moved in his face as he bent over the phone. He wondered why this picture was so precise and so remarkably disagreeable. Sometimes he dreamed with childish satisfaction about what would happen— during a war, after all, bombs were not out of the question—if one day, far behind the blockhouse lost on the brink of a world a prey to spirits and surprises, Varin's telephone were cut.

Toward the end of the week, a warm fog covered the Roof; the German reconnaissance planes stopped coming. Then the weather cleared again, dry and very bright now, and two days of brutal cold paralyzed the plateau: the ice on the road virtually severed the blockhouse from Les Falizes, and the men sulked in the bitter humor of sailors becalmed. The morning of the third day, Grange, shivering as he put on his clothes, was surprised to look out his window and see a man from the blockhouse at Les Buttés making his way through the waist-high snow. Les Buttés was relaying an urgent message from Moriarmé: it was the alerting order—*number one* alert.

"Still there's nothing on the radio," he repeated incredulously. "And besides, with snow like this! . . ." But suddenly the snow meant nothing beside the little square of white paper on Grange's desk, and the radio's silence smelled of a trap; in wartime an order, a piece of news, a simple rumor, suddenly casts the ominous light of an eclipse over everything, and the world swings into a new season. Behind the partition (to make assurance doubly sure, he had ordered a review of their arms) the sound of gun breaches against the raw wood sent the men's bad humor through Grange's nerves. They didn't put much stock in these alerts but found them supremely annoying. It was a kind of forfeit: a whole capital of mild, comfortable daydreams, of security measures saved up and consolidated from week to week, gone up in a puff of smoke: they were starting again from zero. Then, even to its distant heart behind the Meuse, the army shuddered, wondered, seethed with all its awakened antennas. Toward noon, Captain Varin himself appeared in front of the blockhouse.

"Olivon will heat some coffee for you," Grange said, when they had sat down. "Les Buttés relayed the alert this morning," he continued, coughing and grimacing indiscreetly. The captain shrugged his shoulders.

"I don't know any more about it than you do, my friend. But even so, this time, I'd be surprised. . . . We got stuck three times on the way up from l'Eclaterie." He gestured wearily toward the snow-choked road. "Everything in order here?" he continued, almost absentmindedly.

"Those embrasure funnels still haven't come."

The captain shrugged again. Everyone in Moriarmé knew he had been furious for three months over missing equipment: he suffered from these lidless blockhouses as from a mutilation.

"I know," he said, with a bitter twitch of his lips. "I can't make them myself."

He sipped his coffee in silence. "There's something up his sleeve," Grange thought. "Something he's not in a hurry to get out."

The captain put down his cup and unconsciously glanced out the window, like all visitors to the blockhouse; at once the silence of the forest, so difficult to dispel, flowed into the room as calmly as water fills a wreck gone to the bottom.

"Let's go down," Varin said suddenly. The thaw's humid chill became almost intolerable inside the block itself. A few empty bottles rolled across the cement floor near the escape hatch. Through the embrasure, a thin dust-colored shaft of light reflected from the snow outside fell across the raw concrete.

"You should have put something under those munition cases before the thaw," the captain said in his bored tone. "The concrete breeds rust in the winter. God knows what would happen if that alert meant anything!" His eyes fixed on the road through the embrasure, he continued as if he were dreaming aloud: "Everyone's asleep. The less they do, the less they want to do—and as for keeping things greased, the hell with it. There's not one gun in two ready to fire in the whole blockhouse line after this rotten snow."

Grange opened, then closed the breach of the anti-tank gun, which engaged with a delicate, brutal click.

"I'm not saying that for you," Varin snapped. Then,

reflectively: "A percentage. And if it were only the guns that were rusting . . ." The captain slapped his soft leather gloves against his leggings, and insolently raised his chin toward Grange, his nostrils flaring. "A hell of an army, my friend, and it looks to me as if it wants to be an army in hell, before long. All right, it's none of our business," he broke off, resuming the fierce gaiety of tone so characteristic of the man. "Another thing, Grange," he continued after a moment's silence, pulling on his gloves, his eyes lowered: "how would you feel about being transferred to regimental headquarters?"

"Headquarters?"

"To the auxiliary company that's being brought up to strength. It seems I'm more than well supplied with lieutenants since you've come. And they've been nice enough to leave the choice of hara-kari up to me."

Grange looked at the captain and suddenly felt himself blushing. The auxiliary company was one of the best-known soft spots in the service. "It's a little embarrassing," he said after a moment, his voice harsh. "If at least I knew what it was that made you . . ."

"No, Grange," the captain said, putting one hand on his shoulder for a moment. "You don't see what I'm getting at. If the choice were up to me, I'd keep you."

"Then the answer is no," Grange replied, making a sweeping gesture with his finger tips.

"Definitely?"

"Definitely."

The captain frowned and coughed. With the tip of

his shoe he rolled an empty bottle toward the trap door. He seemed embarrassed, undecided.

"There's no point of honor in this business," he said, suddenly turning back toward Grange. "No point of honor. An administrative transfer, that's all. This isn't a post for you, here. You'd be replaced by a non-commissioned officer."

"No," Grange said again, his voice slightly muffled.

There was another silence.

"A woman?" Varin asked, his face producing the wintry grimace that must have been, Grange decided, his *libidinous* expression.

"No," Grange continued after a moment. "Not really."

"Well, then?"

"I prefer staying under your orders."

"No," the captain said, tapping his revolver holster and staring at Grange with a mocking curiosity that melted him a little. "No, not that. . . . That would surprise me."

After inspecting the block, they climbed back up to Grange's room for a moment. The captain gave him a number of documents which he glanced at in passing: for the most part it was the usual singsong, what Grange called "customs": upkeep of blockhouse materiel, tightening of the frontier patrols, installation of the mines and barbwire emplacements. There was one novelty, however: a booklet on how to identify the silhouettes of the German armored units; Grange leafed through it for a moment, suddenly thoughtful again. This time there could be no question of the Siegfried Line: the war was fast growing overripe behind the unchanged official phrases—imperceptibly, with the year, it had changed direction.

"There it is, all right," the captain said, looking over Grange's shoulder. "They're starting to get serious now. . . ." In the captain's vocabulary, *they* never meant the Germans, but merely the stormy peaks of power, the *big chiefs*, against whom he whetted his own mental secession. *At heart, he's on Lucifer's side*, Grange realized, startled by the sympathy that impelled him toward the captain, *only he's a specialist: he sees God with stars on his shoulders.*

"I'm sure you know how late in the day it is," he said. He smiled clumsily; the old *pique* between them suddenly started up again, once more rubbed him against the grain.

"More or less," the captain said, lighting his cigarette with mock calmness. He brushed the notebook off the desk. "And believe me, I'm not sticking my neck out: you'll see them coming with the swallows." They looked out the window for a moment, at loose ends, and drank some more coffee. The noonday sun was already recovering a little strength; the road was mottled with brown puddles. They could hear the snow melting, drop by drop, onto the hencoop.

"Why do you want to stay here?" Varin suddenly asked again. "No," he waved his hand, "please . . . I don't like volunteers, and I know what I'm talking about.

If you tell me you want to fight in the front lines, I'll think less of you, and I won't believe you."

"No," Grange said. "It's something else. I like it here." He felt as if he were hearing the words for the first time, astonished to have known the truth so long.

"Yes, that must be it," the captain said after a moment's silence. He looked fixedly down the road again. "You're a strange man!" he said with an uncertain smile, then stood up to say good-bye and snapped his helmet's chin strap. The mask of his face became handsome and hard again, sharpened by fatigue, the great nose hawklike, the eyes heavily ringed.

"Well, then, I've said what I had to say," he concluded, holding out his hand with something that for the first time resembled cordiality. " 'Having reread, continue,' as they say in indoctrination courses."

" 'Continue,' " Grange said. "I'm not sure you're particularly pleased."

"You're wrong, my friend," Varin said seriously, lighting another cigarette. "I have no objection to fighting the war with men who have found their own way of deserting."

That evening, Grange went out for a short walk. His conversation with the captain had disturbed him, he needed air. What astonished him was the sudden realization he had come to, talking with Varin, of how little Mona counted in his sudden, almost animal desire to stay.

"To live here?" he said, almost aloud. He looked back

through the network of bare trunks at the wretched structure with its long streaks of rust running down the concrete, the little garden littered with tin cans, the rickety chicken coop, and shrugged his shoulders. Here or somewhere else—any quarters were good enough for him. No, it was something else. What most reminded him of his exaltation at Les Falizes, where he seemed to breathe as never before, was the beginning of summer vacations in his childhood—the fever seizing him as soon as he could look out the train windows, still miles away from the coast, and see the trees gradually shrink, stunted by the salt wind—the anxiety suddenly filling his throat at the mere thought that his room in the hotel might not overlook the sea. And the next day there would be the sand castles too, when his heart beat stronger than any-where else just standing next to them, because he knew, and at the same time could not believe, that the tide would soon cover them.

Evenings, once he had sent off several letters, which became more and more of a chore—there were too many barriers to cross to make himself understood—and signed his daily report, Grange went to bed early. He liked to read in bed during the long winter evenings, accompa-nied by the snores that penetrated the thin partition be-tween him and the crew; its key hanging at the head of his bed, he enjoyed feeling the blockhouse around him drifting through the night in marching order, water-tight, closed in on itself like a ship that shuts its hatches. But this evening, instead of his book, he leaned down and picked up the pamphlet Varin had brushed to the floor and turned its pages for a long time. The ponderous gray silhouettes, which he had never seen reproduced before, seemed curiously exotic—another world—with that simultaneously baroque, theatrical, and sinister quality of German war machines which, despite all the requirements of technology, still managed to remind him of Fafnir. "*Unheimlich*," he thought: there was no French word; he studied them with a mixture of repugnance and fascination. Outside, the heavy rain of the Ardennes was beginning to fall with the darkness, its drumming muffled by the snow. Unconsciously, he strained to hear the occasional noises from the crew room, afraid of being surprised, as if he were poring over obscene photographs.

TOWARD the winter's end, Grange's leave came up. Paris, in its brief wet dawn, seemed gray and dirty, unwelcoming. At the hotel he had directed his driver to, the blue-daubed lamps cast a lonely and clinical light across the bed, making the feel of things uncertain. Warmth could be recovered only where bodies were pressed against each other, in the luminous caves of bars and theaters; it was as if the zone of life had gradually, imperceptibly, gone to earth, as in the ice age. Grange ran across a few vague friends here and there, accidental encounters in cafés, but his heart wasn't in it, nor the city's either: Paris was nothing but a great railroad station, a slamming of doors between trains, where all night long the smoky signal lamps winked between the coal-colored rows of houses. At the first signs of spring, no matter how chilly, people were sitting on the café terraces; hands folded in their laps, they watched the city with that idle yet anxious glance one gives one's own house on moving day. Now that the lights were dimmed throughout the city, Paris had lost its bloom, and Grange felt he was touching the hard core: this knot of roads which had been here forever and which shrank, now, between the armies and the country villas, to a city of the Late Empire—its blood thinned to super-numeraries, official stand-ins, and hearing in its own empty streets the murmur of the ambiguous storm that drifted over the frontiers.

Grange was bored: he took another train, this time for the country. The Vienne was swollen by the sudden thaw; a sour spittle flooded the low fields that were already turning green; through the Chinon valley the pale blue of the Touraine was already daubed across every hill; in the naked woods that covered the tufa slopes, flakes and fireworks of yellowish verdure zig-zagged across the bare boughs of winter. He left the inn early in the morning, the Vienne visible on his right, between the still leafless poplars, beneath its long scarves of fog. Suddenly turning into the valley the crisp little town out of the book of hours was revealed at the end of its bridge, its blue-tiled roofs mounting out of the morning's mist more pearly than a school of minnows, and the enormous curtain of the château unfurled above its houses like a royal scroll stretched out at arm's length.

He crossed the bridge with the first peasant carts on their way to market, and early in the morning, sometimes on an empty stomach, drank the light *rosé* of Vienne in a tiny dim cafe, listening to the iron-sheathed cartwheels and the casks rolling over the round cobbles of its steep, narrow streets.

The town did not oppress him: it seemed detached from time, refreshed by some fabulous primitive imagery. A strange unfamiliar light hesitated a moment on this corner of the fifteenth century. The portcullis of the château of Chinon rose: to the sound of trumpets, a great cortège paraded out of its vaults like some fascinating hand from a tarot pack: "*le Prince d'Aquitaine à la tour abolie*," flanked by Bluebeard and the Maid. The world had come apart at some of its principal seams; suddenly his heart leaped up, *possibility* exploded: the highways, for a moment, lay open to the "great undesirables."

What also pleased him was the stone of this countryside, a micaceous chalk that was white and porous, sometimes parched and fissured by the sun, sometimes soft and exfoliated, scaling in the clear pools of water that stood in its declivities, mottled with delicate, smoky grays, gritty blotterlike impregnations, its rough seams scarred with the tiny hardened mildewings of Roquefort. The stone was like a pulpy feminine substance, its skin deep and sensitive, downy with all the subtle impressions of the air. Returning from Chinon, he lingered along the paved bank of the Vienne, his spirits high from his heady breakfast of wine and potted pork, discovering the secret manors of the countryside, safe and sound behind their closed gates, their ancient lawns pierced by deflowered hollyhock stalks—houses wedded supremely to their time, placidly yielding to the gentle, mossy light, like a woman in a garden.

Moreover, the country people never mentioned the war, even pretended not to be particularly interested in it. The stifling atmosphere of Paris, its overparticular anxiety, grew airy here, diverted by those inevitable and inevitably ending natural inclemencies of which peasant wisdom had taken the measure. This war with neither soul nor songs, which had never created a popular mentality, which in each man discreetly murmured *I* and never *we*, imprisoning only the private universe, disoriented the country infinitely less than the city, for here it did not function contrary to the mind's habits: the egoistic, short-run calculation, and the resigned, somewhat magical frequentation of a future evasive by nature. There was nothing changed here, one might have said, beyond a curious rarefaction of manpower; instead of the eve of battle, a mortal conflict, one thought of a country which, in view of a long-term reinforcement, had slowly, ponderously, transported and grafted a massive migration of youth to borderlands a little too exposed. "Odd," Grange thought, "that in this age of lightning wars it should be not an army but a colony that settles on our frontiers. Another year or two and this army will send down roots: it was a sign that already, at Moriarmé and elsewhere, a third of the officers have sent for their wives; I myself . . ."

Sitting at loose ends beside the little wicker table in his bright, sunny room, looking out over the poplars of the Vienne, he fell back into one of his favorite day-dreams about the Roof. Nothing in this war was like any of the others; it was a soft degeneration, a dying twilight of peace indefinitely prolonged—so prolonged that one could dream in spite of oneself, after this strange half-season, this plunge into sleepless nights, each new day attaching itself to the old without any break in continuity. Perhaps for many years now the country would transplant, secrete on its frontiers, a population *de luxe*, a violent, idle military caste depending for its daily bread on the civilians and finally demanding it of them, as the desert nomads levy tribute on the cultivated regions. Frontier prowlers, idlers of the apocalypse, living without material cares on the brink of their sociable abyss, familiars of signs and presages, having no commerce save with a few cloudy and catastrophic grand incertitudes, as in those ancient watchtowers one comes upon at the sea's edge. And after all, Grange reminded himself, sinking deeper into his dream, that too would be a way of living.

From time to time he wrote Mona short, rather child-ish letters. Her resemblance to a plant in the sun, her characteristic openness, her way of growing firm and straight within the grain of life, had straightened him out despite himself: in her radiance, he was no more ashamed of his secret withdrawals than a tree in sunlight of its twisted branches. There was only that strange sensation of falling free, that drifting nausea which became his vice, which he never mentioned to her, from which she remained excluded, and which was yet perhaps the essential thing about her. This was what he called, whenever the faint dizziness began again, "going down into the blockhouse." But when the mere suspicion of the military censors' opening his letters paralyzed him, he understood how nakedly he lived with her.

The last night of his leave, he had a remarkable erotic dream about her. He was hanging on a gallows or a high branch—in any case, at a great height—the sun was shining, yet this posture, though certainly uncomfortable, did not seem to involve any immediate inconvenience, since he was taking particular pleasure in contemplating the sun-flooded landscape and the globed treetops far below. But the heart of the sensual joy that filled him was much nearer: beneath him—so close that at times his bare feet almost brushed against her blond hair—a thin cord suspended Mona by the neck from his ankles. The wind swung both of them gently through the balmy, pleasant air, and from the rope that was strangling Mona, especially when she was shaken by faint convulsions that raised her shoulders, he received—at his bound ankles and also at his neck where the cord took another turn— so exquisite a communication of her naked living *weight* searching, stretching, piercing his body, that he experienced a physical pleasure he had never known before, this ending in the final indecency attributed to hanged men.

The whole morning that followed this strange ecstasy of his dream left Grange floating in a kind of consuming heat, exhausted. And yet it was a dream of love, he decided, strange and poignant, of a really astounding intimacy. The silence and the height, the sea's murmur, were those of the craggy uplands where the wind begins despoiling the trees, or of high cliffs with a view plunging down into the heart of a city.

When he got off the train at Moriarmé, the Roof no longer seemed the same to him. All along the Meuse, new concrete blocks had been poured: here and there, the naked raw gray of their masonry irritated and obsessed the eye. The little town swarmed with more troops than ever. The Meuse front was becoming populous: wherever billetings had interrupted the Roof's solitudes, the cavalry now crossed the river and pushed ahead to the line of blockhouses. On the Roof too, the spring had come, noticeably later than in Touraine, but already brilliant. On the road to the blockhouse, the cool air, washed by the west wind, was delicious: Grange walked between two banks of fresh grass already spreading into the stones of the road, sending up little jets of leaves and birds. Yet this was an odd, unwholesome spring: watching it spread over the Roof scarcely dry from the thaw, he felt it was already jostled, abused by a torrid summer full of the crackle of burning forests that raze the shriveled earth to ash. The spring was coming ahead of

time, exotic as an Easter out of season beneath this sky
that was still cold. Grange looked around him, astonished
by the forest's panic haste; he seemed to have arrived
in an unknown town whose balconies bloomed helter-
skelter, whose streets since dawn were covered with rugs.
It was as if someone were expected.

He found his men glum. The spring was a little too
violent. An almost luxurious divisional rifle range had
been set up behind the Meuse, with moving targets that
rolled along on trucks. Hervouët and Gourcuff practiced
there twice a week with the teams of anti-tank crews
from the blockhouses. "It's something to do!" Olivon
said, his voice sharp and hard. Grange had scarcely returned when the front was again alerted for several
days: the Germans were invading Norway: this time,
there was certainly a thaw! The telephone, which had
now been connected to the blockhouse, summoned him
more frequently to Moriarmé. From early in the afternoon, the precocious heat rose from the sidewalks in
waves along the yellow walls; the little town steamed
in the rancid hollow of its valley. With its offices humming now, its troubled rumors, Moriarmé became in-
supportable to Grange; it was a town breeding pestilence;
he found a little fresh air only on the climb back up to
the Roof, where the shadow of the trees suddenly swallowed the road. When he reached l'Eclaterie, he stepped
off the road for a moment and walked to the cliff's edge.
Before continuing, he sat for a moment on the stone
bench in the already yellowing light. In the center of the

forest's tremendous funnel, clammy with leaden heat and the glaucous light of an aquarium, he could see the little town squatting at the bottom of its valley, incubating in the heat of its grayish stones, and the Meuse moving gently in the green penumbra, like a carp at the bottom of a fishpond.

"What are we waiting for here?" he wondered, and the familiar taste of tepid, stagnant water filled his mouth again. All at once the world seemed inexpressibly alien, indifferent, separated from him by miles and miles. It was as if everything were dissolving under his eyes, disappearing, cautiously evacuating its still intact appearance down the cloudy, sluggish river, and desperately, endlessly going away—going away.

MAY came, and its first hot days immediately burst upon them in ominous, aborted storms that prowled above the Roof all afternoon, caught in the shaggy treetops. Although Varin telephoned him every other minute (the captain played his post commanders like hooked fish—sometimes he even *gave them line*), Grange no longer enjoyed staying in the blockhouse; it weighed on his mind, and he felt free only in the open air. Afternoons, he went more frequently to inspect the progress of the work at Les Fraitures, where the barbwire emplacements were almost finished. As soon as he had the clearing of the upland bogs around him, after climbing the hillside that overhung the last pine groves, the air moving now, and full of high clouds, he felt the sudden relief of the sailor coming on deck from the cramped forecastle. The bog was a thin meadow of peat moss and marsh tea, its rising edges ragged beneath the yellow flames of gorse; occasional puddles of cloudy water lay among the bald patches of this lichen-colored area that smelled of rotting straw. At the end of the bog, where the curtain of low trees closed again, some soldiers in shirt sleeves were driving stakes and laboriously unrolling great bales of barbed wire: faint in the distance came the same spiritless commotion of mattocks, spades, and wire-clippers that clicks and clatters in suburban gardens on a summer night until the darkness falls. Mists drifting across the huge, heavy sky created an emptiness, a strange silence around the tiny amateur putterers pegging out their bean trellises in this Sunday wasteland.

For a long time, Grange stood watching their docile *farniente* in this disproportionate setting against this enormous sky, this endless, oppressive forest horizon, and a vague doubt stirred in the pit of his stomach, an animal suspicion that oppressed him as if some calculation of faces, suddenly conspicuous, had grossly, inexplicably erred as to scale. "They're beginning the siege of Alésia all over again!" he told himself, puzzled. Then he shrugged his shoulders, but unconsciously thought of Varin, and a disagreeable feeling settled somewhere under his stomach, where forebodings knit: as if he must spread a warning, set off an alarm. At one side of the emplacement, a machine gun was hanging from a stake driven into the middle of the bog—stretched out on the grass, his hands under his head, the gunner was whistling happily, his feet at right angles to each other. "They don't have any idea," Grange reflected, glum again and scandalized, and for a moment Varin, the cavalry lieutenant, Norway, the funnels that never came—all coursed together through his mind like the sibilant rout of water flushing down a drain.

One evening, toward the end of the first week in May, when they had finished dinner early, Grange took Hervouët with him to inspect Hill 403, where the engineers had just opened a new cut. The evening was clear, but heavy; there was not a breath of air in the forest. They followed a winding service path bordered with wild strawberry plants, and when they stopped talking they unconsciously strained their ears, surprised by this empty twilight that was open as dead eyes are: it would last until the forest animals awakened. Hervouët scarcely spoke at all: instinctively, through the rank undergrowth, where patches of heavy sunlight fell on grass that was already black, they adopted the long strides and silences of their patrols, when the only noise was the eternal rustle of cold grass against their knees. A curious image occurred to Grange: it seemed as though he were walking in this unfamiliar forest as if through his own life. The world had gone to sleep like another Olivet, exhausted by fear and foreboding, intoxicated with anxiety and weariness, but the day had not disappeared with it: there remained this cold, abundant light which survived all human caring and seemed to glow upon the empty world for itself alone—this abandoned nocturnal eye that opened before its time and somehow seemed to be looking elsewhere. It was still daytime here—a strange daylight limbo laved by fear and desire, a barren brightness that did not warm: the light of a dead moon.

When they drew near the hillock where the cut began, the sky was still quite pale. Along the ruts in the road, filled by the last rainstorm, the slanting light silvered the rails of cloudy water; a smell of sated earth, the coolness of the water-cress pond rose from the banks of new grass. The cuckoo's solitary call came at intervals from the curtain of trees at the other end of the clearing. High up, against the great clouds that stirred the sky, Hervouët pointed to a buzzard slowly circling, barely moving, borne on the exhalation of the warm forest like a piece of burnt paper above a great fire. This motionless vigil added a drop of venom to the forest's ponderous silence. Grange saw that Hervouët was sliding his rifle sling off his shoulder.

"No nonsense!" he said, touching Hervouët's arm: heard anywhere in the forest, a rifle shot brought a mountain of papers down on their heads from Moriarmé.

Hervouët shoved back his rifle with a shrug and carefully spit into the rut. "Gamekeepers!" he said, with a dejected scowl.

"After the war, you can hunt as much as you want. After all, they do leave us pretty much alone here."

"It's not that," Hervouët replied. He seemed hesitant

and puzzled, the look of a whipped dog in his eyes. "Just the opposite."

"You want to get into action?"

"I'm in no hurry, *mon lieutenant*." He shrugged again and looked Grange directly in the eyes. "No hurry at all. Only after a while, it's funny here. . . ." He gestured toward the empty forest and shook his head. "No one's behind us. . . ."

They quickly crossed the cut. The trees were too young here: virtually none of the rough stakes already cut were the proper size—besides, the work was obviously going forward with extreme nonchalance. Near a pile of skeletal branches, a makeshift hut leaned against a tree. They went inside. Three or four quartered logs served as benches: on one was laid, almost emblematically, a deck of cards and two empty bottles, a still life of a war hibernating now in broad sunlight. Grange put his hands in his pockets and glanced around the hut with one of Varin's grimaces.

"The National Workshops," he whistled between his teeth. "After all, when you think what they pay their men! . . ."

He made a dismissive gesture with one hand, feeling quite unperturbed by this sleeping army in its enchanted forest. And in some obscure corner of his thoughts he even recognized a certain complicity. There was a confused but powerful charm in sprawling in this besotted boat that had thrown its helm, then its oars overboard—the curious charm of *drifting with the current.*

They sat on the logs and lit their cigarettes without speaking. A heavy barrage of storm clouds had gathered in the west, where the sun had almost set. From the hut, they could hear only an occasional rustle of leaves, a sparrow flying to its roost, and then quite near a rabbit bolting into the brake. Toward Belgium, the bluish distances were already darkening. A heavy dome of clouds gradually slipped across the sky; at the horizon, a palpitation of heat lightning flashed across the darkness. The evening's calm was not that of sleep: fanned by this distant trembling, it was as if the earth was waiting only for this heavy lid which reached further into the sky at every moment. A few drops splattered on the tin roof, then stopped; a powdery, scorched odor rose from the earth, filling their nostrils with all the heat's intensity.

"Funny kind of spring," Grange said, unbuttoning his collar. "I feel like sleeping out here on the grass."

"I know," Hervouët answered. "I don't feel like going back either."

"We'll go as far as Les Censes de Braye. Take a look at the emplacements there."

As soon as they had turned onto the new path that led to the frontier—a smuggler's trail—they plunged into a green and bitter savor that the oncoming night crushed from the earth, headier than the smell of new-mown hay. Occasionally a cold mist rose as high as their faces, brutally chilling their temples: puddles from the last storm still flooded all the hollows of the path. Above

them, the branches divided to reveal a streak of yellow
sky; the storm clouds had begun to devour it. With the
zigzags of the path, Grange's sense of direction quickly
vanished. A familiar sense of well-being filled his mind;
he slipped into the forest night as if into a kind of freedom.

"We must be there, *mon lieutenant.*"

They heard a tin can clatter. The emplacement cut
across the path here: they had bumped into the wire
before they had guessed it was there. Beyond the frontier, the path ran down toward a shallow ravine; a wisp
of fog was already oozing up, as deliberate as cigar
smoke. The Belgian side rose abruptly, a grass-grown,
deforested slope with a few scattered pine saplings. The
moon had risen, and what the clouds had not yet obscured
of its light clung to this smooth slope, still touched by a
vestige of daylight, and made the clearing beyond the
pool of fog, beyond the dark cones of the saplings, a forbidden and magical site, half fairy ring and half witches'
circle. Behind the hilltop, towards which the meadow
sloped up, there was silhouetted between the trees the
ridge of a low roof—probably a woodcutter's hut.

"Things are pretty quiet now," Hervouët said, nodding toward the roof. "The wire gets in their way."

"That cabin?"

"Smugglers. It's a hideout."

Grange had come to understand why he liked taking
Hervouët along on his night rounds: the frontier fascinated him, and he had learned all its secrets, from the

minutest detail of its crude, ingenious hiding places to the sudden commotion of the forest creatures. Nothing, Grange felt, bound them closer to each other than these whispered conversations, these long silences while their gloved hands groped along the invisible thread of barbed wire, the lifeline that stretched across the leaden night.

"There's no money in it any more," Hervouët said, scowling. "And besides, they're busy other places."

"Called up?" Grange asked mildly, raising his head: he had heard from Moriarmé that frontier crossings were quite rare now.

"Yes," Hervouët answered. "The smugglers, and then the rest. Probably because it looks bad. They've called up a lot recently. Just at Waregnies . . ."

"There still hasn't been an alert," Grange said, without conviction.

"If you ask me, they know something all the same, *mon lieutenant*." Hervouët shook his head. "They're closer than we are. And besides, it's bound to happen. It's the time of year."

They smoked for a moment in silence. The air was lighter now; the clouds disappeared; one or two long rolls of thunder faded behind the Belgian horizon with a pacified grumble. The moon had risen over the forest now: beyond the clearing in the woods, the slope was frosted with a cold, mineral light, spotted by the inky shadow of the saplings on the grass. This evening, as never before, Grange felt he was living in a forgotten wilderness: the whole immensity of the Ardennes throbbed in this ghostly clearing like the heart of a magic forest pounding around its fountain. This slumbering vigil of the treetops disturbed him. He reflected on the strange expression Hervouët had just used: "No one's behind us." What they had left behind, what they were supposed to protect, no longer mattered very much: the lines were cut; in this darkness full of forebodings all *raisons d'être* had lost their hold. Perhaps for the first time, Grange told himself, he was mobilized in a dream army. "I'm dreaming here—we're all dreaming—but of what?" Everything around him was anxiety and vacillation, as if the world men had woven was unraveling stitch by stich. There remained only a pure, blind waiting: the starry night, the forgotten forest, the enormous tide that swelled behind the horizon brutally stripped them all, as the sound of waves breaking behind dunes creates a sudden nakedness.

They talked for a moment about Hervouët's leave—his turn was coming up. The sea would have fallen now at La Brière, Grange decided. He conjured up quite clearly the wide cinder towpaths between the canals, the everlasting mist that hung over the peat fires. He remembered the mysterious sickness, the slow fever that came with the summer, burning deep under the grass with neither flame nor heat, so that you could stir up showers of sparks just by dragging a stick across the peat—the earth was like a dog showing its teeth.

"All that! . . ." Hervouët concluded, almost with indifference. They were unconsciously speaking of the place as if it were some primitive Africa, pleasant to dream of exploring but not to be taken very seriously.

"And you won't be sad about leaving Les Mazures?" Grange asked, touching him lightly on the shoulder.

"There's no one left at Les Mazures any more," Hervouët said, not looking at him. "They were evacuated yesterday." And with a shrug of the shoulders he added, "It's just as well. It's no time for women now."

They walked back in silence as far as the cut. The moon, turning the fog into steam, made it into a vague jungle; on the other side of the widened clearing, the rampart of the forest stood in the cold light, motionless and upright like a man.

"Go on back," Grange said to Hervouët. "I have to stop at Les Falizes."

Mona's light was still on. Grange drummed noisily two or three times on the grating latch; this was his usual way of announcing himself when she wasn't asleep yet. Mona was reading, lying barefoot on the bed, wearing blue jeans and one of Julia's blouses.

"Come sit down." Without getting up, she moved over to make room for him on the bed. Nothing seemed so intimate, so binding, as these blind-man's gestures of hers. "What's the matter, poppy?" she asked, leaning on one elbow, her eyes suddenly troubled.

"The war," he said with an exhausted sigh, familiarly hooking his helmet onto the cupboard key. He felt his heart give a little start: where his helmet always swung for a moment on its chin strap, a tiny curved rut had been worn in the polished wood.

"How silly you are," she cried, pulling him against her mouth. But they quickly broke apart: against hers, his lips tasted of fever, a sour, faded taste.

"Darling, you're sick. It must be marsh fever," she said, seizing his wrist and nodding knowingly. "Julia always says it's *so* bad to go into those bogs on your patrols the way you do."

"No, Mona, I mean it. The war—seriously. You must leave," he said, turning his head, his tone less firm than he would have liked.

"How boring you are, darling!" Mona heaved a little premonitory sigh which he knew quite well by now. It was the sandman's hour: sleep suddenly threw her across the bed, as defenseless as a lamb with its legs tied together. For Mona, sleep was sometimes a subtle form of escape, like animals that *play dead* in the face of danger.

He seized her shoulder and shook her a little. "You must leave, Mona, do you understand?" he repeated, his voice serious.

"But why—what's the matter?" With a sudden thrust of her hips Mona sat up and stared at him, her eyes wild, as if waking from a nightmare.

"Tell Julia." He took her fingers in his, mechanically. "Tomorrow." His eyes were hard and abstracted; he felt time weighing on his shoulders and thought of railroad stations early in the morning, when farewells have a taste of ashes, but when the early wind is so fresh.

He dared not tell her that, light as she was, she encumbered his life, and that he wanted to be alone now.

Mona cried for a long time; heavily shaken against Grange's shoulder, her head was quite sticky with her tears. When the sobbing stopped, they listened together to the noises of the wakened forest that came through the open door, and he felt her gentle plantlike breathing begin again, as if the storm were dripping from her leaves now. "A whole season," he thought, and wondered if he had loved her. It was less and more than that: there had been room only for her.

THE night of May ninth, Lieutenant Grange slept badly. He had gone to bed with a headache, all his windows open, though even the forest night could not prevail against the precocious heat. When he awoke at dawn, it seemed at first as if he had been dreaming heavily: his head was full of a peculiar insistent buzzing. He was aware of a sudden current of cool, wet air streaming over him from the nearby window, but this draft slipped over his face with a particular tonality, musical and vibrant, as if it were woven of a crackling of wing cases. For a moment in his bewilderment he had the pleasant sensation that time had somehow run together, that the forest dawn had mingled with the torrid noon, electrified by the hum of cicadas. The image vanished as he realized that a pane of his window, where the putty had fallen out of the frame, was rattling near his cheek. "It's the window," he told himself as he buried his head in the pillow again, "I'll have to tell Olivon about it." Yet somewhere in his fog, without quite connecting it with this rattling, he also felt a shrill note of panic urgency rising from second to second in the morning air, a kind of gleaming weight in the light, and he also became curiously aware of the fragility, the grotesque thinness of the roof over him which seemed to be flying away. He nestled into his bed, uncomfortable, naked, and exposed to the sound that streamed from the sky, swelling as it approached. Two knocks at his door wakened him completely this time.

"They're going over, *mon yeutenant,*" Olivon called from behind the partition. His voice was strangely throaty, its indifference a little choked, pitched somewhere between incredulity and panic.

The men were already at the windows, barefoot, tousled, hastily buckling their belts. The sun had not yet appeared, but the night was pale in the east, already graying the vast horizon of the Belgian forests. The wet dawn was cold—the soles of his feet were freezing on the raw cement. A great whine slowly rising to its zenith came in through the open windows. The sound did not seem earthly; it involved, rather, the whole vault of the sky, which suddenly became a solid *firmament* and began to vibrate like a sheet of tin: at first he thought of some strange meteorological phenomenon, an aurora borealis in which sound had inexplicably been substituted for light. What reinforced this impression was the response of the night-drenched earth, where nothing human stirred yet which grew troubled, the voices of its creatures raised in confused alarm; toward Les Buttés, in the darkness where sounds carried far, dogs howled continually, as if at the full moon, and from time to time over the low, even whine he could hear rising from the nearby underbrush a muffled, cautious cackle of alarm. At the horizon, a new throbbing wave began to swell, rising slowly toward its calm culmination, flowing majestically across the sky, and this time, suddenly, the dogs were still: there was nothing but that one sound. Then the whine fell, losing its powerful unison, its quality of a seamless wave, leaving behind a trail of coughs, isolated, wandering murmurs, and some cocks crowed in the empty forest across the stupefied and vacant earth, as after a storm: the sun was beginning to rise.

The men felt suddenly chilled, but did not think to close the windows; they waited, ears straining to catch the faint sounds the wind was beginning to carry over the forest. Olivon made coffee. They began a rather heated discussion: Olivon was the only one to maintain that they had been English planes returning from Germany.

"They're after Hitler's fleet, *mon yeutenant*. That's all the English care about—they don't give a damn for anything else."

Grange was always struck by the broad winks the

men exchanged whenever English tactics were mentioned. For them, *perfidious Albion* was still the master of cunning, exemplar of sly double-dealing.

"We'll read about it in the papers," Gourcuff concluded, who, when in doubt, uncorked his bottle of red wine early.

But it was soon clear that the day was not to return so easily to its customary somnolence. Once more a hum swelled on the horizon, less powerful this time, apparently shifting toward the north; suddenly the slow stream of black specks that glided over the forest began to caper about: two, three, four huge explosions shook the morning, and from the belly of the broken earth, in the direction of the distant cavalry billetings, rose the furious cough of machine guns. And this time there was silence in the crew room. A wisp of paltry gray smoke, almost disappointing after such racket, slowly unraveled far above the woods. They stared at it a long time without speaking a word.

"Better get dressed," Gourcuff concluded sagely. The telephone rang.

"Is that you, Grange?" The voice was low, a little muffled, less ironic than Grange would have supposed, despite the commotion in the background: the captain's office was unusually noisy this morning. "I'm sending on the orders for *number one* alert. . . ." Varin's voice emphasized the word with humorous relish. "It'll be confirmed in writing." The voice grew more familiar, almost bantering now: the captain must have got rid of some official visitor. "That was *one*, you know, not *two*—we've still got some discipline around here, even if we fight like customs inspectors. But of course this is only an installment. You've got a radio?"

"No, ours is broken."

"Too bad, my friend, too bad. It's fascinating this morning. They've gone into Holland, Belgium, and Luxembourg." The captain's tone changed to one of advice: "Better send two of your men to the frontier. With tools. The Belgians will lift their barricade this morning. Maybe they'll need a hand."

"I'll send them right away."

The captain did not hang up. "Are you all right?" he asked after a moment's silence, in a new tone in which there was a note of timidity.

"Why shouldn't I be?"

"I mean . . ." The captain suddenly seemed embarrassed, confused. "I mean, after all, this time, it has something to do with you."

Grange felt the news had little effect on his men. The fog of the phony war was lifting now, partially revealing a perspective that was not a pretty one, and all too foreseeable. But there still remained a margin of uncertainty where things could still get stuck, bogged down, extinguished. They would live on that. Belgium, Holland—they were much closer than Norway. But with a little ingenuity they could still keep things vague enough for comfort.

"At least we keep quiet about it," Olivon said, glancing around the room with a proprietary look. "It's not like the cavalry," he added hypocritically. "They'll be slobbering over it all day."

During the first hours of the morning, the morale of the crew room began to rise noticeably. Hervouët and Gourcuff came back from the frontier with canteens of gin and pockets stuffed with cigarettes and little Belgian flags. The burgomaster of Waregnies himself had come to raise the barricade. There were a lot of women. The sentiments of the Belgians strongly impressed the men. The news of the great distant shock had left them stunned: they measured it by the recoil which almost instantaneously struck along the frontier.

"The Boches—they're going to get what's coming to them!" Gourcuff proclaimed, already red, sweaty, and optimistic with wine.

Toward eight, the traffic began to be heavy. Two sidecars and a motorcycle went by, heading toward the frontier at top speed. Then a signal truck and an engineer's detachment. Behind the blockhouse, toward the cavalry billetings, rose the whine of motors. Grange, Olivon, Gourcuff, and Hervouët were sitting on the window sills, their legs dangling against the wall, as if it were Bastille Day. The sun burned brightly, the morning was cloudless. Toward nine, they heard a tremendous series of backfires in the west which slowly turned into a low drone: the cavalry had begun to move.

It was the noise that triumphed over everything; a heavy, terebrating commotion of armor plate, chains, canteens, caterpillar treads, and shuddering metal that snatched at the nape of the neck and did not let go again. The little groups of civilians standing at the roadside—appearing by magic out of the empty woods to watch the procession—raised a few cheers when the first tanks passed, but they soon left off, discouraged: now they were waiting as if for a long freight train to pass; the men on the tanks rode by, mute, indifferent, and almost allegorical, like firemen sitting in rows along their ladders. The sun was already hot on armor plates; the crews were in shirt sleeves, some naked to the waist—beneath their heavy visorless helmets, the sweating faces seemed strangely young, but their youth was worn, feverish, devoured from within, like the young men on threshing machines or mine cars, thrown by loose handfuls into the maw of the machine: rather than the roses on the rifles of 1914, one was reminded of the railroad engineer lifting his goggles from his hollow, too brilliant eyes, of the coal stoker in the bunker. And, as much as the tremendous racket, it was this workmanlike, frightening taciturnity that froze the roadside groups to silence before the strange grease-stained human stream caught in steel up to the waist.

The caravan took a long time passing, its gray dust rolling heavily over the treetops, with whistles, jams, squealing of brakes, and sudden stops that roughly shook the tanks, making the armor plating clatter. And for a long time, the blockhouse crew had not said a word: there was only the hard sun, the stale, dry dust in their throats, the racket of hot steel and the grinding stones of the road. By ten, the tanks passed at longer intervals: the supply and service vehicles, as well as the liaison cars from behind the lines, had to keep to the main highways, which were more practicable. From time to time a few isolated sidecars passed, faster than tanks on the empty road. Grange felt as if the show was over: the civilian groups were ragged now, slowly moving off down the road, still in a daze; as the last tanks passed they waved distractedly, not even stopping, as if to stragglers in a race.

Then there were two long, empty hours. Toward noon, an infantry company came up the road toward Belgium. The men were marching in Indian file oh one side of the road, hugging the shade in widely spaced detachments: they looked, Grange thought, much more as if they were setting out on an adventure. The airplane put the infantry back in an earlier age, reviving the convoy of salt-smugglers, the gay *chouannerie* of the hedge-wars, the warpath of the *Last of the Mohicans*.

Grange offered the second lieutenant of the last section and his already sweating men something to drink; he was suddenly a little ashamed of his too-plentiful cellar. This morning, moreover, he wanted to exchange news with everyone who passed: the road fastened its rumors upon him like leeches. The infantry battalion was to cover the cavalry division: according to the second lieutenant, they would be replacing the latter at the bridges.

"Only they're on wheels and we've got our legs," he

added, his glass in his hand, pink and smiling and a little out of breath. "There's a mess up there, believe me. We're not anywhere near where we're supposed to be."

The men moved on. Their Meuse encampments had been machine-gunned that morning. They disappeared with a curious movement, edging along the trees, their helmets a little lopsided from glancing up so often at the streak of open sky above the road.

During the afternoon, another procession appeared on the road, moving in the opposite direction: the last inhabitants of Les Falizes were leaving to be immediately evacuated from the Meuse stations. There was a gloomy, almost military rhythm in this column with nothing of the sordid pathos of farms abandoned in panic, barnyards full of feathers split from slashed eiderdowns. Besides, there were very few people left at Les Falizes now: the old men and the children had left at the beginning of winter with the heavy baggage—and these last frontiersmen were like the population of an empire's disputed marches for whom the calendar held in store other risks than frost or hail. They withdrew after notice had been given—rather sternly, decorously, without calling the Heavens to witness, without balking, accustomed to abrupt warnings, like men to whom the military authorities have granted a few patches of ground in a rifle range. The women, almost all young, wept quietly, sitting on neat packets of linen wrapped in sheets; the men walked in silence, but with a firm expression, beside their carts; even the Bihoreau boy limped after his donkey, fiercely hammering the road with his wooden leg. Madame Tranet rode in his cart, her hair bound up in a red kerchief: leaning against the side, already soiled by sweat and the jolts of the road, she looked like a Russian *baba*; a veil of affliction and dust the color of the road floated around the thin procession, and it was not only anxiety which suddenly aged their faces; a powerful hand was shaking the dice, they were entering the world of short farewells and vague separations; already the countryside was slipping before their eyes in the faded colors of recollection. Olivon embraced Madame Tranet, but the place and the watching eyes embarrassed him: at the last moment he merely gave her a great smack on the cheek. "The key's next to the door," she said in a low voice, making a sign with one hand. "You know, for coffee. . . ."

Grange shook hands with her in silence.

"After the war, when we've hung old Hitler!" Gourcuff shouted without conviction, but the words sounded like an obscenity and roused neither echoes nor laughter. The procession moved off. Madame Tranet had untied her kerchief; from farther and farther away, leaning against the cartrail, she waved at them. The men walked on without turning back, their shoulders heavy, their gait reconciled to long roads.

The exodus from Les Falizes suddenly cast a pall over the blockhouse, which the cavalry's splendid array had so excited only that morning. Toward the end of the afternoon, a series of muffled, almost subterranean explosions came from the south, very far away; the shock, instead of shaking the window glass, seemed this time to rise from the concrete floor which shuddered like an anvil under their feet: obscure messages, heavy with significance, were passing deep in the bowels of the troubled earth. The men in the crew room ate to pass the time, munching on bread and pieces of chocolate: you could tell the war had actually begun by the sound of grinding jaws that filled the silences. But at the impact of the explosions, they stopped eating and immediately raised their heads toward the sound with an expression of dull anxiety, like a horse looking up from its manger and suddenly pricking up its ears. When the silence returned, after the diminutive earthquake, they heard the birds cheeping in the trees quite near the windows and beneath them the clatter of the empty bottles rolling across the blockhouse floor—and for a long time they listened to the troubled murmurs of the distance with that new ear they discovered deep within themselves.

During the evening, Grange decided to go up to Les Falizes for some bales of wire the engineers had left there: Moriarmé sent orders for the immediate reinforcement of the blockhouse's little emplacement. The last hum of the airplanes had died away; there was a vacant sweetness in the evening air, as if the day were secretly unclasping its armor, relieved of its excessive tension; from far away came the dull hammering of a woodpecker against the oak trunks, and its whinnying call as it flew off into the thickets. The war's tide had withdrawn, but leaving its gray foam hanging from the bushes; on the path to Les Falizes, empty bottles, gasoline tins, and tin cans littered the roadside—the soft asphalt, rolled by the caterpiller treads, was corrugated with tiny gleaming ridges. When Grange stepped into the clearing, the edge of the forest cast long shadows over the meadow; every pane of the rest home's windows gleamed in the warm light. When he reached the first houses, Grange stopped for a moment, suddenly uncomfortable, sat down on a boulder that had rolled into the roadside grass, and held his breath a few seconds. He listened to the silence. It was a flat, stale silence that fell across the honeyed sunlight and seemed to stuff his ears with a soft wadding, like snow. When you took the road here, you suddenly penetrated this silence the way you might fall on the other side of a fence, a little stunned, disoriented, vaguely expecting a hand to be laid on your shoulder.

"Is it possible I'm alone here?" Grange wondered stupidly, and unconsciously turned around, his back tingling with an unpleasant shudder. He looked at the tall, dark, already cool grass in which the boulder was half-buried, the tiny empty road—palisaded with its closed, hostile doors and windows—where the wind noiselessly raised tiny cones of dust. The windows of the rest home darkened now, and the light suddenly seemed to have fallen; a fine powder sanded the gray of the walls: the colors of tiles, shutters, and doors had already faded.

Grange left the road and turned into the alley that ran

behind the houses; he walked to Mona's house between cabbage beds, tiny haystacks, and bean poles. He had not been back to Les Falizes since she had left; mechanically he drummed two or three times against the latch. Again he turned around, seized by a stronger foreboding: a half-dozen white hens had stopped scratching at the haystack and were staring at him, one foot raised, fastening their red eyes on him with a low cackle: it was as if these ignorant creatures, at this twilight moment between night and day, lamented their separation from man in the tones of a secret, wary council. When he raised the latch and pushed the door, it opened easily. With the shutters closed the room was very dark at this late hour; he could see only the little brass table gleaming in the dim air, and the waxed panels of the cupboards barely awakened by the light from the half-open door. The room's incredible disorder was gone: the hammock was folded, the complicated network of string too; an ageless cloistral sadness flowed from these severe furnishings, from the bare walls that smelled of the long winter's dry rot, mingled with the waxy odor of the rough linen piled in the cupboards. A great blue fly wakened on a curtain, surprised by the ray of light, and began to buzz noisily in the heavy air.

"Well, it was here. . . ." Grange thought, frightened. He wanted to go away; the silence pressed strangely against his temples. He was nauseated by this close air, this ancient chalky light that slipped between the blinds and the windowframe. He opened the door wide; a hen

appeared on the sill, thrusting her head forward to inspect the half-darkness, but the rug seemed to bewilder
her; after a moment of perplexity she disappeared
toward her hay with a cluck of disdain. Through the
limpid air he could still hear, at increasing intervals, the
cries of the birds gathering for the night in the cafe chestnut tree. Grange sat on the bed for a moment dreaming:
the bed yielded to his weight with a familiar creak of
its springs; a sudden desire to lie down here seized him,
to turn his face to the wall, forever abandoning thoughts
and dreams. In an hour, the forest night would come in
through the open door with its wild aromas, its wary
noises, absolving this feverish world; he eagerly imagined
the pool of calm, the cool darkness that would filter into
the hollow of the closed house with the night; he felt as if
something inside himself had been desperately choked
off, stopped flowing. His throat closed; he shrugged his
shoulders nervously. The key was still in the lock; he
closed the door, locked it, and put the key in his pocket.
Outside it was still light, but already chilly; a tender,
delicate network of yellow light slipped across the
vegetable beds through the peach and cherry trees.

He easily found the rolls of wire in a padlocked lean-to
behind the rest home. There was nothing more to do at
Les Falizes, but he had no desire to return to the blockhouse: the night would be heavy and uncertain, and the
idea that Varin might have telephoned the blockhouse
depressed him again. He set out on the little road once
more, climbing back up toward Les Platanes, walking

hesitantly. Several windows that overlooked the road had no curtains now; their mute stare both embarrassed and attracted him: he zigzagged from one to the next across the empty street. When he pressed his face against one, he could see, through the uneven little panes set with green bottle ends, the red tiles of the bare floor, the sheetless walnut bed, and on the smoky walls the pale rectangles where the fly-specked mirrors and family photographs had been taken down; sometimes, over the bed, where there was a pale cross, the Easter palm, still fresh, was hanging on a nail or trailing across the gray-striped cotton mattress cover. It was these pale areas on the walls that gave a particular impression of dilapidation: the houses seemed to have surrendered, capitulated altogether, as if a tiny night light had just gone out here, in broad daylight. Occasionally Grange stopped in spite of himself to listen: the birds were no longer scolding now, he could hear only a gentle cheeping in the cafe chestnut tree, and, far behind the house, the thrushes calling at the forest's edge.

From the little gardens, in the motionless air, the odor of syringa, lilac, and wisteria drifted across the road, each perfectly distinct. When he reached the Café des Platanes, Grange remembered Madame Tranet's last words.

"After all, it was an invitation," he decided, plucking up his courage. The umbrella had disappeared, but the garden table and chairs were still there. The chestnut tree, drowned in its diminishing racket of birds, threw a deep shadow across the little terrace, which looked like a scene from a play; the door at the back was only waiting for the moonlight in order to open. Grange went in and after searching the glazed cupboard with his flashlight, picked out a bottle of cognac. Suddenly he felt terribly thirsty; he went to the well and filled a bucket with water. In the abandoned silence, the pulley made a tremendous, incongruous racket: a disapproving cackle awakened in the chestnut tree, but muffled, already nocturnal. "If I stayed here, I'd begin talking to the birds," Grange thought. The western sky remained luminous and yellow; below him, through the blacksmith-shop windows, the schoolroom desks glowed in the watery light like so many little mirrors. He sat back in his chair and comfortably stretched his legs out on the table. A black cat crossed the road, carefully setting down its paws one after the other, stared at him slyly a moment, then, after due consideration, jumped onto the terrace. Grange picked it up by the back of the neck; once on his lap, the animal, which at first tried to escape, began to purr lewdly, like a tiny captive city. Grange drank slowly, feeling a vague exaltation, something of the uneasy ecstasy of "anything goes," a suppressed desire for night plunder and broken crockery, as well as the pure well-being that streamed from the cool evening, and, far beneath, a muffled animal anguish born of this silence that promised the trumpets of Judgment. But the warm little life that slept on his knees reassured him.

"*Mon lieutena-ant!* . . ."

He heard Hervouët shouting for him at the first houses of the village as though from the depths of a dark forest. Together they searched the houses, sometimes using their flashlights in the late twilight, and finally discovered an old wheelbarrow onto which they loaded the rolls of barbed wire. Now that there were two of them, the solitude of the phantom village became quite pleasant: they felt free and bold, ready for adventure, glad to be carrying with them whatever they had. Before leaving, they took another cognac under the chestnut tree. The night had fallen, calm and very clear; above their heads, the tree against the sky was a heavy, irregular cloud of ink casting a darker shadow on the terrace, but through its fringe of leaves and even in its rents twinkled a swarm of stars; they spoke in low voices, peacefully, with intervals of silence; the solitude, the odor of the forest, the velvet shadow of the chestnut tree, the ghostly royalty of this dead village, gave Grange an impression of singular luxury. The earth was wild once more, rejuvenated by an aroma of high grass and night campfires, restoring the fierce moods of an oudoor life; there was a silence that filled his ears; something in man was avenged here, and cheered: it was as if the sky were full of new stars. Hidden in the shadow of the trees, only the red tips of their cigarettes moving, they stared into the blue darkness at the road, the roofs that were beginning to soften in the moonlight. The bats had stopped fluttering around the chestnut tree; from the edge of the nearby forest rose the wood owl's strange challenge.

THE morning of the next day was very still. The road from Les Falizes was empty; the forest returned to its solitude. But the Roof's calm was no longer the same. The time hung heavily; a weight had formed beneath the men's stomachs, a turbulence seized hands and feet alike. No one wanted to sit down—they ate their lunch standing at the window. The air was warm and heavy. The dust of the day before still whitened the motionless leaves; only a film of heat trembled over the road.

Toward the middle of the afternoon, the look of things suddenly changed. A heavy whine rose with the heat from the Meuse, and one after another, almost simultaneously, bouquets of huge explosions burst around the arc of the western horizon. And this time smoke rose over the forest horizon—gray and slow: first three columns, than seven, eight, ten, fifteen. They were not disturbing, not even really sinister. But they were there, unavoidably inflecting the landscape, like a new season; come what might, they would no longer be living without them. A swift hand had run along the Roof's edge, lighting the footlights. "The theater of war," Grange reflected. "Not a bad description." What astonished him was this brutal crescendo, this thundering, rattling way of setting the scene, and then, suddenly, this oblivion, this void—a drunkard who pounds on the table hard enough to break it in two, then foggily tries to remember what he was so angry about.

"Well, still, it's only the Meuse they're bombing," he told himself later, disturbed all the same. "What could be more normal than a bombardment? Why, it would be surprising if they didn't bomb it. The roads, and the Belgian railway—everything's over that way." Puzzled, he looked out of his window at the smoke on the horizon; two or three columns were already fraying out, fading. While he watched an idea stirred in his mind—vague still, but troublesome, stubborn as an odor. He had noticed with some surprise that there had been no troops passing toward Belgium after the infantry battalion. Since the night before, the road had been empty: apparently there was to be no infantry support behind the cavalry.

"That's funny," he reflected. "What are they waiting for? Then . . . Maybe Varin and the battalion have been bombed out." With his compass Grange tried to take bearings on Moriarmé, which seemed to coincide behind the woods with one of the heaviest columns of smoke, but to his surprise he realized he was doing this only for form's sake, almost absent-mindedly. His horizon of awareness was shrinking: from that too he could tell the war had really come.

The men finished laying the rolls of wire. The bombardment had made them sullen, but the work went on all the faster: it kept them from thinking. Between the blows of his wooden mallet, Gourcuff was muttering furiously through clenched teeth. The wire had no barbs on it: the engineers had left only the dregs at Les Falizes; the great nickel-plated rolls, spread in zigzags around the blockhouse, looked like a playground.

"There's something missing, *mon yeutenant*, don't you think?" Olivon asked, when the job was through. He had stepped back a few yards to get a better look, squinting at the shabby structure with a curious expression. "We ought to hang up a sign: BEWARE OF THE DOG."

Toward evening, Moriarmé called to confirm the barbwire emplacement, and ordered them to check whether munitions stocks, rockets, and reserve supplies were at full strength.

"I'm sending up the truck with a replacement rocket-gun," Varin added. "Rocket-guns never work. Nev-er."

In spite of himself Grange imagined the inimitable flaring of the nostrils at the other end of the wire. But the captain must have been interrupted, for Sergeant Prinet took the receiver.

"Did you get bombed?" Grange inquired politely.

"Not much damage, *mon lieutenant*. Some horses. And a few houses. Les Verreries . . ."

"Any news?" Grange's voice was somewhat less detached than he would have liked.

"Nothing definite," Prinet said, after a second's hesitation. "The radio says the Germans have crossed the Albert Canal."

It was strange to discover how much or how little names could mean now. The Albert Canal was far away, in the north. The lower reaches of the Scheldt. The others. . . .

"And toward our lines?"

"No one knows," Prinet answered. "The cavalry is in Belgium."

"All by itself?"

"Well . . . yes, I think so, *mon lieutenant*." Prinet seemed surprised. "No one's ready to move down here. They're all waiting."

Behind Prinet's voice, he could just hear a radio in the office playing *La Brabançonne*. Suddenly, mysteriously, the planet's spasm was exploding here: the sound of the sea when you hold a shell to your ear. Outside, the feathery shadow of a little cloud crossed the road, climbed the wall of trees like a squirrel—and through the open window Grange could hear birds chirping peacefully.

At nightfall, after dinner, the crew sat outside, smoking on the grass near the road: in the blockhouse these days they felt like fish stranded on a beach. Grange remembered how on August 2, 1914, his whole town had gathered on the quay with their dinners on their laps, for a gigantic picnic. Everyone brought chairs outdoors —to be within reach of *signs*. Some one saw a flag in the moon, someone else mentioned a tidal wave that was moving up the river: it was some experiment with a mysterious explosive: *Turpin powder*. The memory was one of the delights of his childhood. They had forgotten to send him to bed that night; the world was in its second childhood.

The conversation turned to the bombings. During the afternoon Hervouët had met a man from Les Buttés who had come back up from the Meuse. There was more damage than they had supposed. Blockhouses along the river had been attacked. The man from Les Buttés said that the planes dived straight toward their target with some kind of terrible siren sounding at the same time. Grange could tell from their faces that the men were particularly affected by the siren. They were scandalized. That hoax, a dirty, nasty trick at such a moment conflicted with some innate, obscure code of honor. It was the symbol of a depraved character, the quintessence of cunning, the one hold not allowed.

"They must be rotten clear through to the bone," Gourcuff said, nodding.

Now, with the darkness, the planes returned over the

Meuse, not bombing this time, but on a lingering prowl, probably photographing the afternoon's fires. Lying on their elbows in the dim, already dewy grass, they lit cigarettes and silently watched the battle for a moment. It was like the last lights of a fair going out on the far horizon beneath the cold stars. From the valley rose a chain of tracer bullets—great, slow bubbles of light that mounted one after another into the night's darkness. Then the short burst of anti-aircraft guns, like the clicking of a roulette wheel.

As THEY were going back inside, the truck from Moriarmé stopped and switched off its lights. The driver cursed the road, which had been cut up by the cavalry. He was still shaken by the afternoon's bombing, but from the snatches of news he dropped they could guess that the atmosphere in Moriarmé had grown heavier. The engineers had pulled all the boats to the left bank of the Meuse; the barges for blowing up the bridge had been put in position; the refugees were camped in front of the station and in the streets, waiting for a train that didn't come, already hungry.

"When the civilians clear out . . ." the driver said, with a grimace. "And even so, in a way, it isn't the refugees so much. Up here, *mon lieutenant*, you don't have any idea. You haven't seen the cavalry wounded go through."

The truck drove off down the road, its headlights on now as it jolted noisily along the service path to Les Buttés. They could follow it far into the calm night from all the clatter it made. The darkness of the forest where its little lights bounced along seemed suddenly greater, vaguer, as bewildering as the sea itself.

Just as Grange was about to get into bed, Moriarmé telephoned, reminding them that all blockhouse garrisons were now under cavalry orders.

"I know," Grange said, a little surprised. "Of course."

"You still haven't received orders?"

"No."

There was a dumfounded silence at the other end of the wire. "All right," the voice said at last, crossly and with great precision. "Call tomorrow morning early if nothing comes through. Call without fail."

Grange stretched out on his bed, bewildered. Something in the unknown voice warned him not to take off his clothes. "What's going on?" he wondered, his head throbbing—"and why does everyone in Moriarmé have insomnia?" At the same time a phrase ran through his mind, a bitter little phrase with a hint of poison in it: "the cavalry wounded." Neither the planes nor the bombs had stirred his imagination—even the Roof suddenly blooming with its columns of smoke still looked a little like a natural phenomenon to him. But with "the cavalry wounded" he was suddenly *touched;* the words opened a valve somewhere, unlocked a door that led to a new country. "Will *that* be coming through here?" he wondered, dazed and slightly scandalized at the same time. He glanced toward the forest and shrugged his shoulders. "The Ardennes?" he repeated to himself, incredulous, as if the word could have reassured him, warded off danger—"The Ardennes! . . ." They would have to be crazy to try. . . .

Toward two in the morning he awakened, shivering in a draft; he got up to close the window. The night was perfectly calm, and yet not quite asleep: looking hard at the slightly darker line of the forest horizon, he could see the sky above waken at long intervals with a sudden, unidentifiable blink of light. It was a quick, isolated flash, with nothing of the soft palpitation of heat lightning; instead it was as if a heavy hammer behind the horizon were pounding out red-hot iron on an enormous anvil with regular strokes. Grange strained his ears for a few minutes to hear the noises of the night: a gentle wind stirred the high branches; from the Meuse came the faint rolling sound of a distant train. Now another blink was alternating with the first, veering toward the right; his heart stirred with vague apprehension, Grange stared at the strange sky that reddened slightly as its lights sparkled over the forest. He turned on his lamp; then, using the outside ladder, he climbed into the half-attic and raised the trap door to the roof.

His eyes swept across the treetops, and the source of the reddish glow suddenly became perceptible: a tiny, very distinct point of light which appeared at long intervals at the limit of the horizon. The languid rhythm, the air's motionlessness, and the silence made him think of a slow drop falling at intervals from the night's vaults in exactly the same place, with that tiny explosion spattering against the tip of a stalagmite—when he looked very carefully, he could see a faint pinkish foam stirring for a moment around the point of the flame. The night was soft and calm; Grange no longer felt the cold; leaning on the edge of the wide-open trap door, his chin in both hands, he watched, spellbound, as slow flame mysteriously oozed up out of the earth.

"It's very far away," he mused, "toward Bouillon, maybe Florenville. But what is it?" From time to time he pulled his blanket closer around his shoulders. Toward two-thirty, the flashes grew rarer, then the strange meteor stopped altogether: the night seemed suddenly close, stifling with the exhalations of its growth. Grange suddenly felt the cold; he climbed down to bed, his mind in a daze. Passing the open door of the crew room, he listened to the men's breathing for a moment. It seemed to make the overly calm night where the sinister lights prowled easier to bear. He felt comforted that they were sleeping so well.

THERE are hours when it seems as if a heavy palm were pressing hard upon the earth, full of darkness, like the butcher's hand as he quickly, gently, strokes the calf's frontal bone before bringing down the felling-ax; and at its touch, the earth itself senses the blow and shrinks: as though the very light had turned sour, the morning winds blowing hot and heavy. No interpretable sign has come, but the anxiety is there, in the suddenly thickened sickroom air: all at once a man feels neither hunger nor thirst, but only his courage draining away, and he begins to breathe heavily, as if the world were weighing on his heart.

"It's Sunday," Grange realized with a joyless yawn, seeing the dawn pale at his window. He had slept badly.

The blockhouse steeped in a silence that was a little oppressive, a silence of stagnant water. Mechanically Grange glanced down the empty road. He felt ill at ease. This emptiness, these sleeping roads unoccupied even by behind-the-lines preparation—it was strange, improbable, somehow magical: a road to the Sleeping Beauty's castle. As he came down the iron staircase he lit a cigarette. The morning seemed mild and aqueous, but on the grass the dew was already very cold; the thought of Olivon's hot coffee almost made him turn back, but he had decided to walk as far as the bend of the road where the engineers had installed a mine field. He thought he would find a sappers' guard post there: perhaps there would be news.

There was no one at all. The road had sagged a little above the mine field, banked with dirt that was too soft; in the caterpillar ruts little puddles had accumulated, darkened now by the overhanging foliage. The two bare ends of the detonating wire, sticking out of the ground, led a little farther and came to an end on a heap of gravel.

"That's funny," Grange thought, puzzled. He sat down on the gravel, distinctly out of sorts. It was as if there were no sounds in the forest for a mile around; he strained his ears toward the birdless treetops, vaguely troubled by this suspect disappearance of man and animal, this site suggestive of desertion. Suddenly, as he was lighting his cigarette again, there was a rent in the motionless air, high above his head: a long, shrill clatter, as if a celestial express train were rushing along its tracks, rattling at top speed around curves: the heavy artillery of the Meuse was opening fire on Belgium.

Then it seemed to Grange that things happened very quickly. He was scarcely halfway back to the block-house when a powerful whine of motors began to burrow and thunder through the forest on all sides at once, with the unceremoniousness of a troop of beaters going into a thicket, and suddenly the whole Roof shivered with the tremendous racket of bombs and machine guns. Grange stood for a moment amazed: the forest was vibrating like a street shaken by the uproar of a pneumatic drill; he felt himself shaken by the vehement, incomprehensible tremors that ran through him, from the soles of his feet and from his ears as well. He rushed off the road down a path where the arches of thick-leaved branches showed only a tiny streak of white sky. As soon as he felt himself out of sight, the racket seemed less overpowering: he realized that it was caused by motors rather than by explosions: there were long quiet spells. Reassured, Grange immediately set out for the blockhouse again beneath the roaring sky, but some ten yards ahead the worn asphalt that paved the road here began to fry strangely: it took him a second or two to realize that he was being machine-gunned: he ran back to where the service path turned off. He lit another cigarette, much more comfortable: the noise relieved him. From time to time the sky overhead, in a roar of motors, was crossed by a sudden flight of black shapes;

there was nothing else to be discovered—when Grange
went as far as the road to peer out, he saw flattened
against the sky, which was lighter overhead, clusters of
thinly scattered planes flying high and quite slowly, as if
they were swimming against a current. What he noticed
was their peaceful, easy movement of fish in water, the
way they had of spreading out so comfortably high in the
air, ignoring one another, like schools of fish that cross
without noticing it, each going about its business at different levels in the transparency of the deeps. It suggested
a serene, nonchalant occupation of the elements, except
that from time to time the brutal racket suddenly broke
out again and rose toward its high point, tearing through
the shoals of air where these soft constellations were
floating.

The planes disappeared as they had come, carried away
by a shift of wind. A stale smell of dust wafted over the
forest. Out of the road, scarred now with a tiny whiplash, Grange picked a great round bullet. The idea that
he had been under fire was disconcerting, a little pre-
posterous. The blockhouse had not been attacked: he
found his men, a little pale, sitting on boxes, glasses in
hand.

"Well now, well now!" Gourcuff was saying, shaking
his head. Olivon filled Grange's glass without a word;
the bullet passed from hand to hand, weighed in their
palms, shiny and heavy. Grange picked up the telephone.
Moriarmé did not answer. He shook the lifeless receiver
for a moment against his ear, incredulous, and quickly

hung up, for the men were staring at him. The line had been cut.

"All right. Clean-up time!" he said, his voice suddenly harsh. "We're moving downstairs."

There was little combustible material in the fireproof upper story. They moved two straw mattresses and some blankets to the blockhouse below, then began carrying down a few pieces of furniture by the iron stairway, but this took too long: tables, chairs, even a little chest, flew out of the windows over the barbed wire. The sound of splintering wood gave them heart to finish the job.

"It's good and empty now," Olivon remarked officiously. "And it looks more natural—for the camouflage, I mean. As though we'd cleared out."

When they had moved into the concrete block, they opened some tin cans and ate a little, but with small appetite. From time to time they looked up, feeling out of place, and sniffed the stale air, dank with the odor of roots and earth that rose from the open hatchway. The black cat Grange had brought back from Les Falizes tentatively rested its paws on the cold concrete before disdainfully taking refuge on a crate. They quickly re-opened the armored door and went back out into the air. As they were sitting down on the grass, a sidecar appeared, leading a cyclone of tanks rolling at top speed along the road from Belgium, followed by infantry trucks, mounted guns, half-tracks, and machine-gun tanks, the paint chipped where bullets had hit; hanging on to bumpers, fenders, wherever there was a place to catch hold, rode a swarm of furiously peddling cyclists apparently standing on the dust of the road, while clusters of refugees crowded the running boards and hoods—even an old butcher's van had been caught up in this wild cavalcade, its rack of swaying carcasses covered by a filthy mustard gray. The procession was heading for the Meuse—an avalanche in a tunnel of dust, the muddy, rumbling stream roaring like a herd of water buffalo running from a jungle fire toward a ford in the river.

"Hey, cavalry—you pulling out?" Hervouët shouted, but his voice was not even meant to carry. The men sat there on the tanks, not turning their heads, not speaking, only twisting the corners of their mouths in the slow, tired grin of a boxer hanging from the ropes.

Suddenly the stream dried up, and then, before the dust had settled, a single machine-gun tank, not moving so fast, its barrel pointing to the rear, lurched by the blockhouse. As it was about to pass, the tank stopped with a squeal of brakes and out of the tower appeared a helmet with a leather strap, then a face with hands cupped around the mouth, shouting in stupefaction toward the blockhouse, "It's no time to show off in there! The Germans are ten minutes behind us."

The tank started up again. Grange turned toward his men: it seemed to him their faces had turned quite gray —suddenly he felt a heavy blow land on his nape—and he mechanically raised his wrist at the man's words;

"what time is it?" he wondered quite stupidly— "eleven?" For the first time that day he looked at his watch.

It was four in the afternoon. Behind the forest, with the dry click of a circuit being cut, the bridges over the Meuse were exploding, one after another.

THEY dashed into the blockhouse and slammed the armored door behind them. There was a moment of panic: their fingers trembled, fumbling, as they opened the ammunition boxes. When the clatter of greased steel stopped for a moment, the only sound was a deep breathing that hissed like soup in a caldron. Grange felt a little faint, his eyes were burning; at the same time, a hard little laugh as dry as it was annoying rose under his ribs, and Grange felt his spirits rise with it.

"This is real *army slapstick*," he muttered to himself, "and we're all part of it"—unconsciously a scowl of grim hilarity wrinkled his cheeks. "With the meat van! Now what do *they* think I'm going to do here?" He felt like putting his hands on his hips. "With my three anabaptists! . . . And the mines didn't even go off!" Somehow this scandalized him more than anything else: vengefully he kicked the instruction folders removed from his files. "Asses!" he thought again, with disgusted impartiality. "Stupid asses!" He would have been unable to say just what he meant: the words were a kind of doting absolution that dismissed the world from all appeal, consigned it once and for all to its old chaos.

When the weapons were ready, Gourcuff filled their glasses from his canteen. Hervouët lit his cigarette, which had gone out, from Grange's: each mouth felt the other suck in the smoke with short, greedy puffs. Then, with the sandbags that were piled in one corner, they finished stuffing the gun embrasure as well as they could. The redoubt suddenly grew very dim; they could no longer hear the noises of the forest; only a thin ray of light flashed down the barrel of the gun: it was as if the blockhouse were sinking into the ground. Grange opened the door wide again: the darkness had become more oppressive than their fear; again they heard the calm sounds of the woods.

"We can see them coming, after all," he said, blinking in the sudden brightness. They listened for a moment to the murmurs that slipped through the open door, as gentle to hear as a cool wind against their faces.

"Can't hear a thing," Hervouët declared, shaking his head. "Not a thing."

The light began to grow yellower. Through the door they could see only the underbrush which reached almost to the blockhouse on this side: a moist, writhing chaos of growth.

"Eagle ferns," Grange thought, "those are eagle ferns." It was as if he were seeing them for the first time. He felt a curious joy at having identified the plant: as if he had called an animal by its name. Again they listened for a long time to the silence that flowed through the door, as warming as a lull in the wind.

"We should fall back," Grange mused, giddy with indecision. "If we stay here waiting for orders! . . . The cavalry that was supposed to *pick us up* must have swallowed its assignment, that's for sure." But he felt no desire to leave: the sun-drenched silence pleased him, and just the thought of Moriarmé with its uproar of sweating and exhausted troops, the merciless grinding of machinery, gave him a fit of nausea. And now that the fog of terror was beginning to dissolve, a tiny, bracing idea began to fill his mind: what luck—after all, what really amazingly good luck—that the telephone was cut.

"After all, it couldn't be clearer," he decided, suddenly relieved. "There are no orders: *they* will have to make a move to send them up to me. No orders, no falling back."

Somewhat hypocritically he added, to comfort himself further, "Besides, if I don't see anything coming, what's to stop me from sending Gourcuff down to Moriarmé?"

He looked at his watch again. It was almost five. The men were now slipping out of the blockhouse one by one, basking in the sun against the warm concrete. The end of the afternoon was very calm; a warm, ripening light already stretched shadows across the road.

"They don't give a damn about us, those cavalry guys," Hervouët said, and spat on the ground.

Grange took a few steps down the road, sniffing at the wind. Toward Moriarmé, as toward Belgium, there was nothing in sight. But once he had passed the blockhouse, it was like emerging from a zone of silence: suddenly, far off but very distinctly, came the heavy roll of cannonfire, rising behind him to the north, from the direction of the valley. Toward Belgium, the silence was absolute, and almost magical: the sun, as far as the eye could reach, gilded the soft undulations of the forest with a stormy yellow that rose, range after range, to the horizon. Grange gestured toward the blockhouse: the four men stood clustered in the middle of the road, slowly turning their heads and listening for the sounds in the wind.

"It's over the Meuse," Hervouët said at last, in a tone of voice that rendered homage to the facts. "From around Les Braux, I think."

And the fear returned, no longer the hot, brutal breath of panic that had catapulted them inside the blockhouse, but a marvelous, almost appealing terror that Grange felt rising from the depths of his childhood— from fairy tales: the terror of children lost in the woods at twilight, listening to the faraway branches crack beneath the dreadful heels of the seven-league boots.

They waited. Once they had picked it out, the rumble

of cannonfire filled their ears wherever they were: there was nothing else to hear; it was as if all life in this corner of the earth were escaping, leaking toward that one awakened site. On each side of the road, the forest walls hid the columns of smoke: when Grange put his fingers in his ears for a second, all he could see down the road was a gentle May afternoon already warm under the golden haze, marvelously flowing toward the blue distances. As the moments passed, Grange felt braced by unreal security, a paradoxical result of the battle's giant strides which had overstepped them. The air grew deliciously cool; the filmy light, slanting through the late-afternoon forest, was so rich, so unaccustomed, that he had a sudden, irresistible desire to bathe in it, to steep his limbs in the coppery glow.

"What's to stop me?" he asked himself, with another burst of vague jubilation. "The bridges are cut. I'm alone here. *I can do what I want. . . .*"

He lit a cigarette and with his hands in his pocket began to walk down the middle of the road. "Stay there," he shouted back at the blockhouse. "I'll take a look." The cannon had begun rumbling from farther away now; there were long silences when they could hear the crows resuming their racket in the oak trees. "There's probably not more than one French soldier east of the Meuse by now," Grange thought as he walked along. "Who knows what's happening? Maybe nothing at all!" But at this notion, which seemed almost plausible to him, Grange's heart beat with dim excitement; he felt his mind floating high on the waters of catastrophe. "Maybe nothing at all!" The earth seemed fair and pure to him, as it must have been after the flood; two magpies alighted together beside the road ahead, looking like fabled creatures, carefully smoothing their long tails on the grass. "How far could I walk like this?" he wondered with astonishment, and it seemed to him that his eyes pressed against their sockets to the point of pain: there must be *faults,* unknown veins in the earth, into which he could vanish for once and all. At moments he stopped and listened: he could hear nothing for several minutes; the world seemed to go back to sleep, having shaken itself free of men with a sluggish wriggle of its shoulders. "Maybe I'm on the *other side,*" he mused happily; never had he felt so close *to himself.* He began to whistle and took off his helmet which he swung beside him from its chin strap, like a basket; now and then he touched his pistol butt in its unbuckled holster; all sense of danger had faded, but the touch of the weapon cooled his finger tips; he encouraged this strange new sense of self-suf- ficiency, of carrying everything he possessed on his back. "With a cane in your hand! . . ." He thought of Varin with a burst of gaiety, then the memory of Mona surged through his mind with the perfume of the May forest: he was beginning to understand what Varin had guessed in his own way, what she had released in him without knowing it: this need to cast off his moorings one by one, this sense of unburdening, of profound frivolity that made his heart leap up—a command to *drop every-*

thing. "I've been tied by a rotten thread all this time," he decided with a low laugh. From time to time he kicked a stone ahead of him. "The forest," he thought again. "I'm in the forest." He couldn't have said anything more than that: it was as if his mind were yielding to a better kind of light. Walking was enough: the world opened gently before him as he advanced, like a ford through a river.

"There are no Germans," he suddenly said aloud, shrugging his shoulders and raising his index finger before him, his voice ripe with the wisdom of drunkards. He felt a little like a drunkard, in fact, staggering now because suddenly every *axis* passed through him at once: legislator and judge, invulnerable, redeemed.

He passed near the mine field and continued on toward the frontier. The slope of the road now concealed the blockhouse. The cannonfire had stopped; the silence was complete. Here, where the forest grew higher, shadows already covered the road, but above the treetops the bright sky ran on, more inviting in its soft escape than anything on earth. Between the ruts, a patch of grass had invaded the road: the forest seemed to close over it more densely. Grange felt pressing against his shoulders an unknown wind that rose over this uncertain, lawless earth, open wider than the night's imaginings.

"I'd just have to keep going," he mused, his head whirling, with a gesture that was almost an assent. Again his gaze plunged down the road; this time he thought he saw a tiny shadow moving in the distance and then dis-

appearing again: a man, or an animal, had just disappeared into the underbrush with a timid, agile hop.

He cocked his pistol and walked on. The man had
not run any further: probably at the end of fear and
courage, he was crouched behind an ash-bole almost at
the edge of the road, chin on knees. On the other side of
the tree that half concealed him he stuck out his head
and stared in Grange's eyes without even making a gesture of escape, his squirrellike eyes inflamed and watery.
There was a terror so naked in these round, red, apparently lidless eyes that the man seemed tiny and imponder-
able: one might have picked him out from behind that
tree trunk with one hand.

Judging from his face, he was a tramp, a poacher, or
perhaps one of those Flemish laborers who carry their
lunch over their shoulders in a sack through the beet
fields of Picardy; the sack, the patched jacket, the old
hobnailed boots, certainly indicated that he was no
stranger to the life of the roads. Grange realized that the
retreat must have forced out of its dens a whole curious
tribe who found themselves homeless without making
much of a fuss—the way the rain floods out the snails.
The Belgian seemed only half-reassured by Grange's
uniform: evidently fear of the enemy coincided with another, older, fear of the police. This somewhat disquieting survivor of the fogs did not displease Grange: at
such a moment he had no desire to listen to anyone's
whimpering.

The man had run away from his village, near Marche,

the morning before. A German armored detachment had set fire to it soon after.

"With *rapid-fire cannons!*" the man declared, his throat dry and his Adam's apple bobbing up and down. The use of such an astounding weapon seemed to take his breath away. But the rest of his story was uncertain; his professional discretion revealed only traces of what must have been a private, game-stocked route, a cross-country circuit strewn with chicken feathers. It seemed he had met no one.

"Fantastic!" Grange wondered, astonished. The touch of the incomprehensible void that widened around him made him even more enthusiastic: he flung himself into it. Deep within himself, he admitted to doing so a little complacently: he was combatting what was agonizing with what was unheard-of.

They walked back to the blockhouse, talking calmly. The sun had set now; the night was already gathering in the shadows. Grange did not want to let his Belgian go; impulsively, he offered to put him up for the night. "It's quiet around here," he declared with a briskness less and less assumed, "and thank God we've more than enough. Besides, it's getting dark." As they walked on, he made a number of remarks to his Belgian companion full of a detached optimism, slightly light-headed: the war, Grange said, had its ups and its downs, but what mattered was knowing "how to take it or leave it"—here, anyway, everyone was in a good mood.

"It takes more than what's happened around here to

shake up old soldiers!" he whispered in his companion's ear, winking and pinching his arm. The Belgian began to glance at him sidelong with an odd expression. As they walked on in the gathering darkness, Grange waved his handkerchief toward the blockhouse, fearing a random shot; at the end of the path he could guess three pairs of eyes keener than those in a crow's-nest were watching, and this notion stirred him. "I'm bringing something back," he thought, "but neither crow nor dove." The darkness around them was beginning to black out the ground altogether. Occasionally he glanced at his companion, who seemed to be floating rather than walking beside him on the road, his gait singularly light. It was a scarcely human presence—rather that of a peculiar bat fluttering here in the twilight that rose over the earth. Grange felt perfectly calm. The world seemed no longer inhabited save by dead souls—faint and light as the tongues of fire hovering over the marshes; the time for *questions* had come to an end, the day had died away. "It's really very late," he thought, almost placidly. "Between night and day . . . but it's not such a bad time. You can see better than you'd think."

He found his garrison not so much nervous as hungry. It seemed to Grange that Gourcuff was already almost drunk. They took advantage of the remaining light that still floated beneath the trees to eat their dinner. An unsteady table and two or three chairs had survived the shipwreck of the house above; they fished them out of the underbrush and dragged them behind the blockhouse, where the branches shadowed a tiny weedy lawn, almost within arm's reach of the road. The silence of the forest had become ghostly—for a long time now the rumbling of the cannons·had stopped entirely—above them, the foliage grew heavier and darker; but from the cut of the road, to the right, where the gravel gleamed in the last twilight, filtered a strange gray light the color of stone. When night had fallen, they set two empty bottles on the table and stuck candles in them: the air was so still that a thin thread of smoke rose straight up into the branches over the flame; masses of leaves lit from below emerged vaguely from the darkness; a vestige of ashen light still floated over the road, like the midnight twilight of the North.

When the meal was over, they sat around the table smoking over their empty glasses. It was beginning to grow cooler now. Only the Belgian continued to scrape at his plate; at intervals, astonished by the silence, he glanced up at one or another of the men with his rodent's eyes, as if he were expecting a kick while his mouth kept busy at its own work. Grange supposed there was not one light in the forest from here to the Meuse; he lit one of the candles that had gone out with his lighter; the tiny oval of flame formed again around its dark heart. The gleam must be visible from far away down the road, he mused, and darkness would be much safer; they wanted no one to come now. But he had no desire to put out the candles that drew the four naked faces out of the night, long, ashen shadows moving across them as though they were running down a corridor of wind-blown curtains. Grange liked these faces.

"The hell with it," he repeated to himself almost careless now. He knew that a ground swell had just swept over the earth beyond them, but beneath him he felt only the gentle backwash and the sudden intoxication of his own lightness—they were beached here, a little dazed, in the silence of a forbidden garden. Again he felt an almost voluptuous, dizzying nausea. "I'm not answerable for anything now," he told himself, and his eyelids flickered two or three times. He thrust his hand into his pocket and felt the key of Mona's house. A great livid moon rose slowly over the forest as he watched; its slanting beams glowed on the road, the rough gravel bristled with sharp shadows, becoming a stream bed once again. Nothing seemed more important now than to be sitting beside such a stream, at the heart of the earth's deep labor. He felt a sudden revulsion at the pit of his stomach, as if he had run into the sea across a cold beach: he recognized the fear of being killed; but a part of himself stood aside, floating on the current of the buoyant night: he felt something of what the passengers in the ark must have felt when the waters first lifted it off the ground.

GRANGE took his turn on guard toward three in the morning: he decided that dawn would be the critical hour, and he wanted to have some time to prepare for it. The blockhouse door was still ajar: here the dark concrete face opened on a crack of ashen night that seemed to be painted on the wall. Gourcuff and Olivon were sleeping side by side on the straw mattress—in the corner where the escape hatch was, the glowworm of Hervouët's cigarette gleamed near the floor; at regular intervals the dull tap of an invisible finger knocked off the invisible ash. Grange felt cheated: he did not want anyone to be awake beside him in the darkness. The silence was like a night stop in a railroad station sonorous with frost; It was very cold. He pushed his shoulder against the door, which swung open noiselessly, and deep in his throat tasted the fog like clean linen: the night, steeped in this heavy mist, dissolved gently, motionlessly, toward the dawn.

He unscrewed the top of the thermos standing on a cartridge case and poured himself some hot coffee: the gleam of his flashlight awakened long shiny ovals on the anti-tank shells standing against the gun carriage; it looked as if he had emptied out a basket full of bottles. The flash-light beam traveled over the low ceiling, the dust, the oozing walls. The bitter fog that slipped in from the forest hung in drops on the faint light; his tongue stirred —his mouth tasted of rot. "It's a funny kind of den!" he thought, surprised afresh by the look of their cellar; he squinted his eyes and pressed his lips together: his stomach was turning and he felt the sweetish, muddy dregs, the low tides of courage, slosh within him. He put out the flashlight: at once his anxiety faded a little; he realized that the night still *held* around the blockhouse, as a heavy snowfall holds—but the black chill made his teeth chatter: he was seized with a panic urge to bury himself deep in the warm mattress, his shoulder close beside Gourcuff's.

"That's a good start!" he murmured, and sat down warily on a crate: he felt a kind of soft dizzying undulations sliding through his brain. "The best thing is to breathe deeply a few times," he decided, throwing back his head with ponderous gravity, and he began exercising, when a sudden, terrifying thought began whirling through his mind: *Twelve kilometers*. Twelve kilometers this side of the Meuse! . . . A tide had washed over him that snapped his every hope: *it was impossible*—with lunatic precision he reviewed the events of the day before; certainly somewhere there must be a gap—an order misunderstood—a paper misplaced: "A court martial on top of everything," he thought, shivering as if he were naked. "That's a good one!" He wanted to cry, to run away. But he felt it was not so easy. Deep in his heart he heard a tiny, cheerful—impertinent—wind blowing, the wind that makes the dead leaves dance on the roads at the beginning of winter.

He switched on his flashlight again and made a quick inspection of the blockhouse. Everything seemed to be in order: the gun was pointed toward its night marks—on a crate next to the automatic rifle were piled some thirty refills; in a corner, the shiny heap of cartridges glistened helter-skelter, as if a wheelbarrow had been knocked over. He decided to check the escape tunnel for the last time. Noiselessly, he moved back the hatchway: the dirt steps were hard, reinforced with boards whose edges caught on his heels; at the bottom of the tiny flight of stairs he plunged along a short gallery clean-swept beneath its wooden coffering; some twenty yards farther began an inclined ramp leading to the open air, its opening camouflaged by pine branches: he needed to be alone now, at this hour of the dawn. "I've got to wake up Olivon in twenty minutes," he reminded himself soberly—"two of us will hardly be too many: chances are the Germans will come through early." Yet the image of the war did not fill his mind; he might have been hidden in a tranquil convent, wakening in a sea of white veils and the unreal fog of ground-glass windows; he was only a man crouching at the mouth of a forgotten lair watching the dawn slowly fade the darkness of the forest —again he wondered why *staying* seemed so extraordinarily important to him.

"What is there between the war and me?" he wondered, and felt himself engulfed for a moment in a strange abstraction. "That isn't the question." His mind grew aware of a fresh, daybreak murmur: as if suddenly a noise, a hum, imperceptible as long as it was habitual, had stopped confusing his life. "It began last night," he reflected, "when I started walking down the middle of the road with my hands in my pockets. The Germans are going to come, but I'm not really answerable to anyone. Who could have thought it was so easy to get gack to the sea again?" He raised his coat collar against the piercing chill: drops streamed from the branches down the back of his neck. "But it's still a bad spot to be in," he murmured, with a grimace that pursed his lips. Grange realized now that the end of his adventure was fast ripening behind the curtain of fog, that the silence of the forest was becoming more improbable from minute to minute. He had not stopped being afraid. Yet if French troops had appeared on the road just then, if some reinforcement had come to the rescue, he would have felt cheated.

Grange came out of the tunnel and took a few steps

as far as the edge of the road, ducking to avoid being lashed by the branches. The night was gradually losing its walnut-husk color; the road ahead of him stretched out in a soft milky way that seemed to float between the trees. When he was standing in the middle of the road, the silence became even more obsessive than that of the underbrush, suspended, it seemed, over a bottomless void, almost ceremonial. Grange began to understand why a lost troop of men instinctively marches into cannonfire: the emptiness of a field of battle was a kind of disequilibrium, like an affiction of the ears; the world without sight or sound lost its moorings, sinking, deaf and blind, through layers of soft sargasso weed.

"The Meuse!" he thought suddenly. "What's happening on the Meuse? The Germans must be farther than Moriarmé by now!" In his imagination, the war continued on its own momentum, following in the furious wake of the routed cavalry. "We must be in a kind of pocket here. . . . Maybe the war is over," he thought. All these possibilities jostled together at once, but gently; he felt scarcely concerned, watching the thread of yellow smoke from his cigarette separate itself from the pale cotton wool of the fog. "This must be the dawn," he decided with a tiny prickle of delight; he remembered that the day begins when a soldier can tell a white thread from a black one. The earth still swam in a greenish pool of oil that was over a man's head, but the treetops were sharp now against the pale sky; a few feet away, he made out a denser clot of darkness, which was the outline of the blockhouse. The calm was absolute—the silence and the chill at the dawn's heart gave the light a strangely solemn tinge: this was not daylight penetrating the earth, but a pure anticipation not of this world, the gaze of a half-open eye across which floated the hint of an intelligible meaning. "A house," he mused, as if he were seeing it for the first time, "a single window looking down a road where something is supposed to happen."

"IT MUST be almost five," Grange decided even before looking at his watch. The shadow of the clustered oaks now reached all the way across the path. The waning day's first stir of air did nothing to cool the blockhouse, which continued steeping in its rancid humidity, but the day itself grew heavy, hesitating at the moment of its decline. When they looked out through the embrasure, there was nothing but the road's rough ribbon of slag to see, beneath shadows that were already longer. Silence had seized the forest again; every now and then a faint breeze rustled the branches.

"It's like a railroad with the tracks taken up," Grange thought. "We've been cut off. . . ."

He remembered hearing of outlaws who gave themselves up, a need stronger than hunger luring them out of hiding to buy the newspaper. For hours now the men had been prowling inside the blockhouse like caged animals.

"You take over," he said to Olivon, handing him the strap of his field glasses. "No one outside till I come back. I'm going to take a look toward Les Houches."

As soon as he stepped out of the concrete block, he was struck by a wakened, vibrant animation of the air which did not penetrate through the narrow embrasures. Grange walked half bent over under the arching branches across a stretch of grass and thick moss, trying not to step on branches that would crack; he began to hurry. The sunny afternoon was much less asleep than they thought in the blockhouse; the forest itself cocked its ears for a distant murmur from the low crest to the north—the ground, though padded by moss, reverberated at intervals with a faint shudder. Every ten yards or so, Grange turned and glanced suspiciously at the empty thickets: this pocket of calm half-light around him was becoming venomous, like the shadow of the manchineel tree.

"If only you could see something!" he thought. Suddenly this shadowy solitude made him feverish; he would have given a year of his life to tear away the curtain of branches, spread the bars of the green cage, around which the earth was catching fire.

Before turning down toward Les Houches, the path paralleled the crest of the plateau for about a hundred yards, running toward Les Buttés through a grove of pine saplings where the forest seemed to spread a little. The horizon was still hidden behind the branches, but a lively, already cool breeeze from the north swept the crest and carried sounds with it. Despite the sun, the place was dark and gloomy—at the foot of a pine, water dripped from one of those moss-grown stone troughs that recalled Shakespeare's Arden, restoring the Roof to a still more primitive savagery. Once he was on the plateau itself, the wind carried through the pines a kind of broad, dark murmur, a confusion of heavy vehicles interminably lurching down torn roads, that seemed to fill the whole of the northwest horizon.

"It's not so far from the blockhouse as I thought," Grange decided. "It even might be . . ." He strained to hear, curiously stirred. The open space, the long slope of the plateau that tilted, he guessed, behind the vault of branches, toward the north, for the first time gave the battle a panoramic character: the sense of danger, the fear of solitude disappeared in the feeling of a new scale: a face of the earth was at grips with the fire of heaven. What he might think of it was not very important. Only, if you listened carefully, above the ground base of massive corrosion—that collapsing cliff attacked by the waves—you could distinguish a nearer sound that cut across the forest toward the road from Les Houches: a continual throbbing of motors and behind that a jolting dance of clashing metal, as if enormous plates of tin were slowly being dragged over a rough pavement. The caterpillars.

"There they are!" Grange told himself, growing pale and stepping behind a tree. He felt a little dizzy; incredulously he stared around him at the forest's absurd opera decor. A bewildering feeling of *let it go at that* paralyzed his arms and legs. The stream of iron crawled on its way, peaceful, lulling, interminable: in a kind of daze, he watched the cavalcade pass.

Walking back to the blockhouse, he whistled to warn his men. As soon as he stepped off the crest, the clatter of machines, the battle's racket, stopped as if by magic. A faint mist of heat still trembled over the road where a dozen crows were pecking in the sunlight, laced now by the shadows of branches. The image of the enchanted castle, the sheltered *island*, occurred to him again, unconsciously comforting him with a wild hope.

"You can't tell much," he said, back inside the blockhouse. "They're bombarding along the Meuse. Anyway," he added a little too quickly, shrugging his shoulders, "we'll know before nightfall."

Soberly, they took turns drinking from Gourcuff's canteen and resumed their posts. Without a word Olivon shook the last drops out onto the concrete. "*They know*," Grange realized, startled. "Or they've guessed. My voice." Despite himself, his heart felt a little lighter.

Another half hour passed. There was a subtle silence in the blockhouse now, the silence of keen eyes, which weighs less than that of straining ears—it was the silence of a workroom absorbed in delicate needlework. Every now and then, Grange, finding it difficult to focus his

binoculars through the narrow embrasure, nudged
Hervouët and put his eye for a second to the gun sight:
nothing stirred in the block's half-darkness save this sly,
childish war of elbows. The light was turning yellow.
The road slag, which had glared during the afternoon
through the tiny aperture, now became quite soft and
pulpy in the distance, like sand on a beach; the evening's
nuances appeared one after another with an almost Chi-
nese delicacy, as if in a darkroom. A thin hyphen drawn
by an agile, cursive hand, crossed the white road and disappeared into the grass: a marten. There was another
moment of calm silence. Then, all together, the crows
flew off, like Wotan's crows, and a clear rumble, gay in
the gentle evening air, wakened down the road.

"Ready!" Gourcuff shouted, almost bayed, at
Hervouët.

The noise was in no hurry to reveal its source: it took
its time. They could hear the driver changing gears as
he took the invisible slope of the rise, and something unexpected in the sound, something too light, too fast, made
Grange slip his hand into his pocket, nervously fumbling
for the booklet of silhouettes.

The truck suddenly appeared, much farther away than
they expected: a dark, slender silhouette half swallowed
up by the trembling of the road. Slender and delicate—
delicate. At first it grew larger though remaining perfectly immobile, then, as it gradually descended the slope,
it headed for the side of the road and stopped in front
of the mined trench with the somewhat comical per-

plexity of an ant testing the danger of a plank's under-side.

"The bastards!" Olivon whispered, dumfounded.

"Ready!" Hervouët breathed; his eye glued to the sight, he stroked the range finder wickedly. "*It's a green.*"

The truck, having satisfied itself as to the obstacle, began moving very slowly, and suddenly lurched into the ditch more heavily than they expected. "No *sightseeing bus*," Grange thought. On smooth terrain now, the truck rapidly grew larger, straight and dark in a kind of bellicose, bullish charge—*levantando*—as if it were breathing fire. "Now!" Grange thought. A last terrible hesitation twisted his stomach, but two inches from his cheek he saw Hervouët's mouth slowly opening.

"Fire!" he whispered.

The shot left the gun with such brutal force that Grange, lying alongside the barrel, thought the impact had crushed his shoulder. A kind of cough shook the truck, which suddenly spat out of its hood a bouquet of long paper streamers, then turned off toward the shoulder at the right, digging up the ground a little as it plunged but not overturning, coming to a dead stop against the trees.

"Right in the kisser!" Gourcuff growled, his teeth clenched, and with the furious explosion of a motorcycle warming up in a tiny garage, he emptied half a machine-gun belt into the wreck.

In the circle of the binoculars, behind the smashed windshield, the seat seemed empty, but the branches hanging down over the road kept Grange from seeing it distinctly. One of the front tires had been torn open. In any case, the first glance settled all questions: the truck was dead, dead the way a man can be dead, already a prey to the weeds, subject to a livid discoloration that must have been the dust of the shattered windshield; it looked like a fly wrapped up in a spiderweb. The carnage left Grange with sweating palms; he felt a cold bar against the back of his neck and smelled the bitter fume of sweat that rose from Hervouët's jacket. Gunpowder prickled sharply in his nose and the clichés told the truth: it was intoxicating.

"Go take a look," Grange ordered Olivon. "Out the hatch and through the woods. We'll cover you."

Soundless behind their reloaded weapons, they followed Olivon's silhouette which threaded its way between the branches, moving with a dreadful slowness: they felt like giving him a push. The air had grown cooler; the splotches of sunshine disappeared from the road one by one. The silence that had fallen now was the petrified silence after the explosion of a slap: they sensed that a cold, enormous rage was gathering somewhere before exploding.

"It's not so much as if we were going to be killed," Grange reflected, moistening his dry gums with his tongue. "It's strange—it's more as if we were going to be *punished*."

Through the binoculars he saw Olivon jump into the rear of the truck and then run back to the blockhouse along the road.

"There are two men," he gasped, out of breath. "Young . . ."

He tossed two gray-green shoulder tabs onto the cartridge case and two heavy, old-fashioned revolvers and a few pale gray lumps the color of cardboard: rye *knackebrot* that crunched in their jaws with a stale, sharp taste—sorry food.

"No," he added, a little shamefully, "there weren't any papers."

"And the stuff in back?"

"They must be account books, *mon yeutenant*," he answered, looking embarrassed. "Boxes full of account books." In a lifeless tone he added: "There must be enough for a whole division, that's for sure." They stared at each other, dumfounded.

"Shit!" Hervouët finally whispered, furious. A vague, appalling ghost of the *sacred* suddenly appeared in the forest, conjured out of the depths of the army barracks: they had laid hands on the *arcana*. No one could foresee the consequences.

They uncorked a bottle of the *réserve* and went back to their posts. The atmosphere was heavy now, the red wine weighed in their stomachs. The bitter smell of powder filled the humid air of the block. The last slanting ray of sunlight climbed up the forest wall on the left side of the road and disappeared; suddenly the whole landscape shifted in the cool evening air. Then, once again, without hurrying, like a wasp's nest slowly wakening, the distant hollow of the road sent up a second rumble. And this time a terrible shudder seized them all. The invisible humming filled the evening—even the woods around them seemed to become uncertain, hostile, suddenly swarming along all the hidden paths.

The sound of the motor died before it reached the crest, but almost at once another picked it up. Behind the short rise of the road, sometimes shrill, sometimes deep, the venomous humming of the secret meeting did not stop again.

"Maybe they've set up a cross-country shuttle. That's what they must have done—cross-country . . ." Grange strained to hear, stupidly, desperately, trying to convince himself that the rumble was heading off toward the left. All at once a heavy, brutal hail lashed against the concrete, and Grange, staring through the embrasure, suddenly saw a cluster of sparks rise out of the earth and spread in all directions through the branches, dragging a scratchy, agonized caterwauling behind them.

"God!" Olivon said in a hollow voice, "tracer bullets," and again they heard nothing in the block but their own harsh breathing.

"Send out a squirt," Grange snapped nervously at Gourcuff.

Gourcuff shook his head. In the half-light, he was *steaming* in front of his machine gun, like an old horse. "Can't see. . . !" His voice was a childish, terrified whimper.

"The trees in back—spray there!"

There was no time. A dim shock that echoed in their

chests, a dry, massive combustion smashed against the blockhouse, followed by cascades of tinkling broken glass. In a second, the sandbags stuffing the embrasures fell away and a sudden sinister whiteness swept across the whole concrete block. Facing the naked daylight that burst in upon them, the last thing Grange saw was Hervouët, a little pale, edging backward step by step toward the rear wall, as if an angel were pushing him by the shoulders against his will.

"Time to b——"

"*It's inside!*" Grange thought. "No, it's outside. . . . No, it's inside." There wasn't that much smoke. When a violent whiplash had wrapped around his calf and thigh, he had instinctively thrown himself to the ground, almost gently, like a boxer rolling with the blow. He didn't feel very seriously hurt. He looked up through the dust that filled his throat at the grayish concrete roof, pitted now with clear round holes, as if a mattock had struck between its ridges. He felt only an emptiness in his head and a coolness at his temples—he was very near fainting, wanted to faint, and then, strangely beyond fainting, experienced a relief which was the comfort of a page turned, and the day over.

GRANGE pushed Gourcuff toward the hatchway; halfway down the stairway, he turned for a last look around the blockhouse. Since the shell had exploded, there had not been one moment of panic. He felt somehow invulnerable. Olivon and Hervouët were laid out on the mattress; the overcoat thrown over them was too short: rather than leave the faces covered and the feet showing, which seemed to Grange like some hideous joke, they had pulled the coat down over the feet. And in order not to see the faces any more, they had turned the bodies on their flank, side by side, faces toward the concrete wall. Grange felt the two identity tags in his pocket—he had taken them off their wrists and could hear them clinking against another piece of metal:

Mona's key. The blockhouse was a chalky wreck where Grange's feet stumbled over pieces of twisted iron; the plaster dust was already whitening the folds of the over-coat, filling the hollows with a sordid snow. Something about it infuriated Grange: he hoisted himself out of the hatchway again, shook the coat furiously, and laid it over the bodies up to the shoulders. Then he slipped into the tunnel without turning back and pulled the hatch closed over his head.

As they came out of the tunnel, there still seemed to be light in the undergrowth. They used Grange's compass and plunged through the forest toward the west. The sound of motors had started on the road again—behind them, toward the blockhouse, loud voices shouted to each other through the woods, calm and relaxed, like hunters when the shoot is over. They walked on, bent double, through the dense tangle of May branches, leaving a noisy wake of broken boughs. But they paid no attention: the voices behind them gradually faded out; the sense of strange, almost intoxicating immunity that fills prisoners and wounded men persisted. Occasionally they stopped for breath and drank a mouthful out of Gourcuff's canteen. All their thoughts now began to flow of their own accord down another slope. The war was continuing, but was already moving far away, with the diminishing sound of the last drops of a squall that dry up on the windowpanes.

"What are you going to do, after the war?" Grange asked, almost without thinking.

They talked as men talk on a railroad platform in wartime, their minds elsewhere, when a change of trains will break off indifferent farewells.

The terrain ahead of them began to slope gently: they were approaching the ravines of Braye, which ran out not far from the blockhouse after gashing into the plateau above. The forest in this area was a thick tangle of chestnut saplings; walking here, brushing aside the rubbery stems, became exhausting; Gourcuff's rifle continually caught on the branches; he swore; their coats hooked on brambles; the bayonet sheath clanked against the canteens with the muffled ring of a herd coming down from the upland pastures.

"We'll never get there," Grange thought, almost casually. "Besides . . ."

His leg was beginning to swell and grow heavy. He stopped to change the bandage and threw the bloody rag into the bushes. When he put his weight on his heel, a sharp spear of pain leaped up to his hips; he drew a long breath, his eyes closed, and wiped the tickling sweat off his icy brow; two or three stars were already twinkling in the treetops. The sounds of voices and motors had stopped. The blood he had lost left him floating, lightheaded, in the calm night. They were walking toward the Meuse. But it didn't matter now whether they reached the Meuse. It didn't matter where they were. Against the harsh cloth that bound his skin, he felt the faint velvety shudder of fever, still almost voluptuous.

"Stop," he murmured to Gourcuff, tugging at his

bayonet sheath. The clanking gave him gooseflesh. "I'm thirsty."

There was nothing but red wine in their canteens: scarcely had he tasted the sharp stuff this time when a fit of nausea twisted his stomach, as though he had swallowed sawdust. He tried to stand up but his leg gave beneath him, suddenly filled with needles. He lifted his trouser leg above his hard, swollen knee that was mottled with pale bluish spots. "Probably a splinter I didn't even feel," he thought. He leaned against a chestnut sapling, his leg straight out before him on the moss. Another stream of icy sweat trickled down his forehead. Putting his hand under his belt to unbuckle it, he pulled it away sticky with blood: he had been hit in the hip as well.

"It's bad," he said sharply. "Leave me here."

He looked at Gourcuff planted before him, his legs wide apart as he corked his canteen, his mouth wide in a perplexity so comical than Grange felt a ghost of laughter slip across his face without moving it, as if at a distance. The clumsiness of a man dealing with wounds suddenly struck him, yet at this moment he would not have wanted a woman with him. "Go on," he continued, angry now. "It'll be night soon." He held out the compass. Gourcuff stood motionless before him, his head down; with the toe of his shoe he kicked at twigs on the moss, his expression undecided. The darkness was falling fast now, their faces were already indistinct.

"I'd just as soon stay here," Gourcuff said at last, with a grimace that looked as if he wanted to cry. He was holding the compass at arm's length, clumsily, like the saucer under a cup of coffee.

"Don't be stupid. Get out of here. You'll get caught here without doing any good at all. *That's an order*," Grange added, and felt that in spite of himself his tone was vaguely burlesqued. Again he had the sense that this war, in its least detail, was imitating something without being able to decide what it was.

After a few seconds, Gourcuff shook his head, filled a canteen with wine, and left it on the moss next to Grange; he poured several handfuls of biscuits out of his knapsack onto a piece of newspaper. Then he leaned Grange comfortably against the chestnut tree and spread his blanket over his legs. Grange guessed that he was delaying on purpose. When he found nothing else to do, he sat down beside the chestnut tree, his legs crossed. They lit their cigarettes with Gourcuff's lighter. The darkness was upon them; for precaution's sake, they held their helmets over the tiny red points that glowed already in the darkness.

"All right, *mon lieutenant*, if that's the way you want it," Gourcuff said, after they had wished each other good luck. "If I find any of the guys over there, we'll come back for you," he added modestly.

He began moving off behind the trees—a floundering, noisy mass gradually vanishing into the dimness of the thicket. From time to time he stopped and turned around, and Grange guessed that he was glancing back with the

JULIEN GRACQ

panic look of a dog that is frightened at no longer being called back.

He listened for a long time to the crackling of the underbrush that grew fainter now, swallowed up by the forest like a stone in a well. As long as he kept completely still, his leg hurt him very little. The coolness that followed the twilight was not yet unpleasant. Mechanically, he chewed a piece of biscuit, then spat it out: the pasty flour stuck to his tongue: he was thirsty again. Above him a trace of greenish light still lingered between the branches: over the forest fell the stupefied calm of the first moment of darkness, before the night birds wakened. At this moment, the animals were not yet aroused—only the woods: occasionally a branch moved after the heat of the day, drawing after it a languid feathery rustling, the sound of gardens after rain.

"How empty it is!" he thought. Memories turned in his mind, images of a strange earth without men—winter wanderings in the forest, afternoons in the blockhouse when all he could see from his window were the warm drops of the thaw swelling one by one at the tips of the branches. The earth slipped away beneath him, alien and incongruous, like a night train whose clatter suddenly rises, rushes toward the horizon, and fades into the landscape. Lying at almost full length on the ground, the cold began to take him, but at the same time an inexpressible calm filled his mind.

"I'm really here," he told himself. It occurred to him that the war was lost, but the thought came calmly, list-

206

lessly. "I'm demobilized," he mused again. Suddenly he realized that Les Falizes was close by. The image of a lair, a hiding place, became an obsessive one; he remembered that all wounded men drag themselves toward a house. There was a well of fresh water, a deep well, near Mona's house. The anticipation of that black water moistened his throat; he felt the cold, delicious touch on his mouth. "I'll try in a little while," he decided. "But not now, not right away. I have to get back my strength."

He nodded once or twice in the darkness, pleased with having reasoned so well. The path to Les Falizes must pass nearby, somewhere to the east. But where was the east? He remembered that he had given his compass to Gourcuff: a sudden, wild, stubborn anger made him tremble against his tree: two or three great tears of rage ran down his cheeks. But his mind drifted despite himself, slipped its moorings: he supposed Olivon and Hervouët would be decorated: no one could say—no one—that they hadn't defended the blockhouse.

Posthumously, he reflected. The formula mechanically turned round and round in his mind: it seemed somewhat abstruse, but important, imposing, like those seals on old official documents that fastened down a bow of silk ribbon. His fever seized him again; he realized that if he waited any longer he wouldn't be able to stand up any more. He drank a little wine out of Gourcuff's canteen and stuffed some biscuits in his pocket; then he cut a branch overhead with his pocketknife and made it into a cane. After a few moments' effort, he managed to stand up: so long as he did not bend his knee, he could use his wounded leg, as if it were a wooden leg. A dog bayed to his right; he moved toward the sound through the thicket, and, a hundred steps farther, came out into the path to Les Falizes.

A haste, a childish anxiety, drew him onward now, forcing one step after another, his stiff leg stumbling in the holes of the dark path. He was making for the house as if he were expected there. When he stopped, his forehead throbbing with fever, dripping with sweat, he cocked his ears again in the silence of the forest, surprised at this world that would let a man escape like water through a pile of sand. When his neck began to feel weak, he threw away his helmet: the fresh air did him good.

"No one here!" he repeated to himself. "No one!" Once again he felt like crying; his heart contracted. "Maybe I'm going to die," he thought. His mind wandered despite himself, burdened by an increasing heaviness: now he remembered that gangrene began in infected wounds; the maddening certainty seized him that his leg was turning black: he stopped, lay down on the ground, and began to roll back his trouser leg. "I've forgotten my flashlight," he suddenly realized, and again a furious, impotent rage shook him with sobs: leaning forward in the darkness with oxlike stubbornness, he tried to bring his eye closer to his leg, straining his aching hips. He felt he was about to faint—the cold sweat trickled down his forehead—and lying on one side he vomited tiny mouthfuls of the red wine and biscuit he had swallowed. Yet as soon as he was prone and motion-less again, he felt only a little pain, his strength returned —a sense of tranquility, of stupid happiness, filled him, as though he were floating. "Or as if I were convales-cent," he mused. "But from what?"

He remained lying on the ground for at least an hour. There was no hurry to start off again; he looked at the branches above him that stretched over the path against the paler sky: it was as if the night that lay ahead of him down this corridor was inconceivably long and peaceful —he felt lost, really lost, far from all paths: no one was expecting him any more—ever—anywhere. This moment seemed delicious to him. When the cold began to be un-bearable, he stood up almost easily. The path grew harder beneath his feet now, wakening the deep muffled echo of an empty room; he was in the village before he noticed it: here the long, blind walls of the barns fused with the forest. Turning into the little alley where Mona's house was, he stopped to listen a last time. The stiff rooftrees of the houses silhouetted against the night seemed to make it clearer, emptier. The silence was abso-lute, but it was no longer the silence of the forest. It was a widowed silence, full of the sad, sealed nuance which the overhang of stone walls gives the night. Only to the right, where the clearing opened a little between the hamlet and the forest, the gardens roused by the froth of May seethed against the dark houses in a slow, breath-ing tide that stirred the dark air and seemed to swell be-

neath the starry sky; at intervals, from the other end of
the village, the dog began baying again—the sense of
gentle, magical tranquility that had filled him on the
path seized him once more.

In the alley, he suddenly felt at the end of his strength
—he had thrown away his cane and was clinging with
one hand to the fence posts, with the other he was already holding the key wrapped in his handkerchief; the
odor of the gardens made him dizzy. "I'm coming," he
thought, "I'm coming back!" His teeth were chattering,
the key trembled in his hand less from fever than his
wild haste; from time to time he seized his wrist with
his left hand, trying to suppress the continuing jerks. "I
couldn't open it," he thought, and supported his heavy
head with one hand. "I couldn't." Yet he had strength
enough to close and lock the door behind him, and then,
in the thick darkness, he moved into the room, hands held
out before him, struck his knee against the side of the bed
and fell backwards upon it, his legs wide.

He lay motionless for a long time waiting for his breath
to come back; his heartbeats grew calmer. A faint gray
light filtered into the room now, through the transom
over the door and the hearts cut in the shutters. The
counterpane yielded softly under his weight; he felt he
could snuggle here as if inside a womb; the silence
seemed marvelous to him, varnished with a faint odor of
wax, purified by the salubrious, bitter perfume of lavender. His body gradually revived in this black silence—
his strength was restored.

"What a business!" he thought. He still felt a little dazed, but he tried to pull his thoughts together; he realized that once he had closed this door a line was drawn, an epilogue had been pronounced: his brief wartime adventure had come to an end. What surprised him was the void created around him: a ghostly, yawning, stale void that drew him in. He had sent Mona away. Olivon and Hervouët were dead. Gourcuff had gone. The war was shifting far away, very insignificant now, already devoured by these dim, heavy shadows that came back to crouch around him. He looked about him, still stunned by the shock of his wound, watching the heavy waters of the closed room floating beneath the moon, crushed by the silence of the countryside. "What a move!" he thought. He tried to remember, wrinkling his forehead, what it was he had watched for from his window, waited for all winter long down the distances of the road so feverishly, with such morbid curiosity. "I was afraid, and yet I wanted it," he decided. "I was expecting something to happen. I had made room for something. . . ." He knew something *had* happened, but he felt it had not been real: the war continued to hide behind its ghosts, the world around him went on draining away in silence. Now he remembered the night patrols along the silent frontier, from which he had returned so many times to this bed, to Mona. Nothing had *taken shape*. The world remained evasive, kept the cottony, limp feel of hotel rooms under the dim blue night light. Lying on the bed in the darkness, in the hollow of the empty house, he became again the blind prowler he had been all winter, gliding still over a vague twilight border, the way you walked along a beach at night. "Only now I'm touching bottom," he reminded himself with a sense of security. "There's nothing else to wait for. Nothing else. I'm back."

"I mustn't strike a light," he remembered. He stood up, groped for the table, found the pitcher in the bowl and took a long drink; he felt the fine, stale film of dust slipping over his tongue and remembered that it was less than a week ago that he had left Mona. Then he stretched out on the carpet and washed his wound. The water flowed onto the floor without a sound, vanishing into the thick pile. The cold liquid burned, but once he had bathed the wound it seemed as if the pain had dulled a little: he stood up again and drank some more. A faint gray shadow seemed to come toward him from across the room and make him a sign; he raised his hand: the shadow in the mirror repeated the gesture with a drawn-out slowness, as if it were floating in layers of water; he leaned over until his nose was almost pressing against the mirror—but the shadow remained vague, eaten away by the darkness: life did not connect with itself: there was nothing but this approximate confrontation with a dim shadow he could not really make out. Yet thoughts occasionally drifted through his mind which now seemed infinitely remote: he wondered if Gourcuff had reached the Meuse. "Varin was right about the funnels," he decided impartially. But all that didn't matter to him. Nothing was happening. There was no one. Only this stubborn, dim, intimidating shadow that gloated toward him without meeting his own limbo—this ear-splitting silence.

Fatigue throbbed through his skull; his mind reeled with heavy somnolence. He stretched out again on the counterpane without undressing, one leg bare: the silence closed over him like a pool of water. He remembered how he used to listen, sometimes, lying next to Mona while she slept: he thought about her for a moment more; saw again the rainy road where he had met her, where they had laughed so when she said "I'm a widow." But even this image faded: it was as if it were rising despite himself, into more buoyant waters. "Lower," he told himself, "much lower. . . ." He heard the dog bay two or three times, then the cry of the screech owl at the nearby edge of the forest, then nothing more: the earth around him was as dead as a plain of snow. Life fell back to this sweetish silence, the peace of a field of asphodels, only the faint rustle of blood within the ear, like the sound of the unattainable sea in a shell. As he turned over heavily, Grange heard the identity tags clink in his pockets; he wondered what Olivon and Hervouët had bought with such mortuary coin. "Nothing, probably," he decided. He lay for a moment more with his eyes wide open in the darkness, staring toward the ceiling, perfectly still, listening to the buzzing of the blue fly that butted heavily against the walls and the windows. Then he pulled the blanket up over his head and went to sleep.

TITLES IN SERIES

For a complete list of titles, visit www.nyrb.com or write to:
Catalog Requests, NYRB, 435 Hudson Street, New York, NY 10014

* *Also available as an electronic book.*

PAUL BLACKBURN (TRANSLATOR) Proensa*
CAROLINE BLACKWOOD Corrigan*
CAROLINE BLACKWOOD Great Granny Webster*
RONALD BLYTHE Akenfield: Portrait of an English Village*
NICOLAS BOUVIER The Way of the World
EMMANUEL BOVE Henri Duchemin and His Shadows*
MALCOLM BRALY On the Yard*
MILLEN BRAND The Outward Room*
ROBERT BRESSON Notes on the Cinematograph*
SIR THOMAS BROWNE Religio Medici and Urne-Buriall*
JOHN HORNE BURNS The Gallery
ROBERT BURTON The Anatomy of Melancholy
CAMARA LAYE The Radiance of the King
GIROLAMO CARDANO The Book of My Life
DON CARPENTER Hard Rain Falling*
J.L. CARR A Month in the Country*
LEONORA CARRINGTON Down Below*
BLAISE CENDRARS Moravagine
EILEEN CHANG Love in a Fallen City
EILEEN CHANG Naked Earth*
JOAN CHASE During the Reign of the Queen of Persia*
ELLIOTT CHAZE Black Wings Has My Angel*
UPAMANYU CHATTERJEE English, August: An Indian Story
NIRAD C. CHAUDHURI The Autobiography of an Unknown Indian
ANTON CHEKHOV Peasants and Other Stories
ANTON CHEKHOV The Prank: The Best of Young Chekhov*
GABRIEL CHEVALLIER Fear: A Novel of World War I*
JEAN-PAUL CLÉBERT Paris Vagabond*
RICHARD COBB Paris and Elsewhere
COLETTE The Pure and the Impure
JOHN COLLIER Fancies and Goodnights
CARLO COLLODI The Adventures of Pinocchio*
D.G. COMPTON The Continuous Katherine Mortenhoe
IVY COMPTON-BURNETT A House and Its Head
IVY COMPTON-BURNETT Manservant and Maidservant
BARBARA COMYNS The Vet's Daughter
BARBARA COMYNS Our Spoons Came from Woolworths*
ALBERT COSSERY The Jokers*
ALBERT COSSERY Proud Beggars*
HAROLD CRUSE The Crisis of the Negro Intellectual
ASTOLPHE DE CUSTINE Letters from Russia*
LORENZO DA PONTE Memoirs
ELIZABETH DAVID A Book of Mediterranean Food
ELIZABETH DAVID Summer Cooking
L.J. DAVIS A Meaningful Life*
AGNES DE MILLE Dance to the Piper*
VIVANT DENON No Tomorrow/Point de lendemain
MARIA DERMOÛT The Ten Thousand Things
DER NISTER The Family Mashber
TIBOR DÉRY Niki: The Story of a Dog
ANTONIO DI BENEDETTO Zama*
ALFRED DÖBLIN Bright Magic: Stories*
JEAN D'ORMESSON The Glory of the Empire: A Novel, A History*

ARTHUR CONAN DOYLE The Exploits and Adventures of Brigadier Gerard
CHARLES DUFF A Handbook on Hanging
BRUCE DUFFY The World As I Found It*
DAPHNE DU MAURIER Don't Look Now: Stories
ELAINE DUNDY The Dud Avocado*
ELAINE DUNDY The Old Man and Me*
G.B. EDWARDS The Book of Ebenezer Le Page*
JOHN EHLE The Land Breakers*
MARCELLUS EMANTS A Posthumous Confession
EURIPIDES Grief Lessons: Four Plays; translated by Anne Carson
J.G. FARRELL Troubles*
J.G. FARRELL The Siege of Krishnapur*
J.G. FARRELL The Singapore Grip*
ELIZA FAY Original Letters from India
KENNETH FEARING The Big Clock
KENNETH FEARING Clark Gifford's Body
FÉLIX FÉNÉON Novels in Three Lines*
M.I. FINLEY The World of Odysseus
THOMAS FLANAGAN The Year of the French*
BENJAMIN FONDANE Existential Monday: Philosophical Essays*
SANFORD FRIEDMAN Conversations with Beethoven*
SANFORD FRIEDMAN Totempole*
MARC FUMAROLI When the World Spoke French
CARLO EMILIO GADDA That Awful Mess on the Via Merulana
BENITO PÉREZ GÁLDOS Tristana*
MAVIS GALLANT The Cost of Living: Early and Uncollected Stories*
MAVIS GALLANT Paris Stories*
MAVIS GALLANT A Fairly Good Time *with* Green Water, Green Sky*
MAVIS GALLANT Varieties of Exile*
GABRIEL GARCÍA MÁRQUEZ Clandestine in Chile: The Adventures of Miguel Littín
LEONARD GARDNER Fat City*
WILLIAM H. GASS In the Heart of the Heart of the Country: And Other Stories*
WILLIAM H. GASS On Being Blue: A Philosophical Inquiry*
THÉOPHILE GAUTIER My Fantoms
GE FEI The Invisibility Cloak
JEAN GENET Prisoner of Love
ÉLISABETH GILLE The Mirador: Dreamed Memories of Irène Némirovsky by Her Daughter*
NATALIA GINZBURG Family Lexicon*
JEAN GIONO Hill*
JEAN GIONO Melville: A Novel*
JOHN GLASSCO Memoirs of Montparnasse*
P.V. GLOB The Bog People: Iron-Age Man Preserved
NIKOLAI GOGOL Dead Souls*
EDMOND AND JULES DE GONCOURT Pages from the Goncourt Journals
ALICE GOODMAN History Is Our Mother: Three Libretti*
PAUL GOODMAN Growing Up Absurd: Problems of Youth in the Organized Society*
EDWARD GOREY (EDITOR) The Haunted Looking Glass
JEREMIAS GOTTHELF The Black Spider*
A.C. GRAHAM Poems of the Late T'ang
JULIEN GRACQ Balcony in the Forest*
HENRY GREEN Back*
HENRY GREEN Blindness*
HENRY GREEN Caught*

HENRY GREEN Doting*
HENRY GREEN Living*
HENRY GREEN Loving*
HENRY GREEN Nothing*
HENRY GREEN Party Going*
WILLIAM LINDSAY GRESHAM Nightmare Alley*
HANS HERBERT GRIMM Schlump*
EMMETT GROGAN Ringolevio: A Life Played for Keeps
VASILY GROSSMAN An Armenian Sketchbook*
VASILY GROSSMAN Everything Flows*
VASILY GROSSMAN Life and Fate*
VASILY GROSSMAN The Road*
LOUIS GUILLOUX Blood Dark*
OAKLEY HALL Warlock
PATRICK HAMILTON The Slaves of Solitude*
PATRICK HAMILTON Twenty Thousand Streets Under the Sky*
PETER HANDKE Short Letter, Long Farewell
PETER HANDKE Slow Homecoming
THORKILD HANSEN Arabia Felix: The Danish Expedition of 1761–1767*
ELIZABETH HARDWICK The Collected Essays of Elizabeth Hardwick*
ELIZABETH HARDWICK The New York Stories of Elizabeth Hardwick*
ELIZABETH HARDWICK Seduction and Betrayal*
ELIZABETH HARDWICK Sleepless Nights*
L.P. HARTLEY Eustace and Hilda: A Trilogy*
L.P. HARTLEY The Go-Between*
NATHANIEL HAWTHORNE Twenty Days with Julian & Little Bunny by Papa
ALFRED HAYES In Love*
ALFRED HAYES My Face for the World to See*
PAUL HAZARD The Crisis of the European Mind: 1680–1715*
ALICE HERDAN-ZUCKMAYER The Farm in the Green Mountains*
GILBERT HIGHET Poets in a Landscape
RUSSELL HOBAN Turtle Diary*
JANET HOBHOUSE The Furies
YOEL HOFFMANN The Sound of the One Hand: 281 Zen Koans with Answers*
HUGO VON HOFMANNSTHAL The Lord Chandos Letter*
JAMES HOGG The Private Memoirs and Confessions of a Justified Sinner
RICHARD HOLMES Shelley: The Pursuit*
ALISTAIR HORNE A Savage War of Peace: Algeria 1954–1962*
GEOFFREY HOUSEHOLD Rogue Male*
WILLIAM DEAN HOWELLS Indian Summer
BOHUMIL HRABAL Dancing Lessons for the Advanced in Age*
BOHUMIL HRABAL The Little Town Where Time Stood Still*
DOROTHY B. HUGHES The Expendable Man*
DOROTHY B. HUGHES In a Lonely Place*
RICHARD HUGHES A High Wind in Jamaica*
RICHARD HUGHES In Hazard*
RICHARD HUGHES The Fox in the Attic (The Human Predicament, Vol. 1)*
RICHARD HUGHES The Wooden Shepherdess (The Human Predicament, Vol. 2)*
INTIZAR HUSAIN Basti*
MAUDE HUTCHINS Victorine
YASUSHI INOUE Tun-huang*
HENRY JAMES The Ivory Tower
HENRY JAMES The New York Stories of Henry James*